The Passion of Thecla

Faith and Fortitude

The Passion of Thecla

Faith and Fortitude

First Female Christian Missionary and Evangelist

A Speculative Story Based on Historical Records

EDWARD N BROWN

CRYSTAL SEA PRESS
CHICAGO, IL

THE PASSION OF THECLA
Faith and Fortitude

Copyright © 2020 by Edward N Brown

Scripture quotations in this work are taken from:
The New American Bible, Revised Edition, Copyright © 2010, 1991, 1986, 1970 by the Confraternity of Christian Doctrine, Washington, DC, and are used by permission of the copyright owner. All Rights Reserved. No part of the New American Bible may be reproduced in any form without permission in writing from the copyright owner. This is the default citation source unless otherwise noted.
The Good News Translation® (Today's English Version, Second Edition) [the 'Good News Bible'], Copyright © 1992 by the American Bible Society, Philadelphia, PA. Used by permission. All rights reserved. Bible text from the Good News Translation is not to be reproduced in copies or otherwise by any means except as permitted in writing by the American Bible Society.

ISBN: 978-1-7338271-8-8
Library of Congress Control Number: 2019921261

Published by Crystal Sea Press, Chicago, IL
CSP
Printed in the United States of America

For information about this title, or to order other books and/or electronic media, contact the publisher at: www.crystalseapress.com

To all those who are curious about:

The First Female Christian Missionary and Evangelist

The First Female Christian Martyr

The First Christian Feminist

The First Christian Hermitess and Ascetic

The Teenager who became a Saint

This book is a story – a story based on multiple versions of accounts, first circulated broadly by word of mouth, and then written down sometime in the second century. It is a story that revolves around two characters: a great man who became a legend and a saint, and a great woman who has long lingered in obscurity.

The great man is Saint Paul, the Apostle. The setting is his First Missionary Voyage to spread the Gospel to the Gentiles. The year is 47 AD. What happened there stunned the world forever!

This is the story of the faith journey of a young girl

A story of passion, courage, and fortitude

Her lifestyle choices would become legendary

Her exploits would become renowned

She would become a saint

But her name would fade from history

IN THE BEGINNING was the Word,
  And the Word was with God,
  And the Word was God.
He was in the beginning with God.
All things came to be through Him ...

John 1:1-3

GLORY BE to the Father,
  And to the Son,
  And to the Holy Spirit.
  As it was in the beginning,
  Is now,
  And ever shall be.
  World without end.
Amen.

The Gloria Patri
A Catholic Hymn of Praise
(also called The Minor Doxology)

CONTENTS

INTRODUCTION

THE POWER OF THE STORY

IN some ways, the age-old act of listening to stories is a lot like examining the nature or operation of physical objects, looking at and perceiving images (moving or still), or contemplating and reflecting on abstract notions (such as mathematics or literature). The imagination is stimulated, the mental models are mesmerizing, and the excitement is captivating. You are immersed in an alternate reality, like a fantasy or dream.

Now, there are some special stories that hold special power over all of us. Ancient stories of faith and mysterious stories of hope – creation, covenant, good and evil, virtue and vice, life and death, resurrection and salvation – stories of how others before us dealt with the concepts, and coped with the dilemmas. These are the stories that affect our souls – stories that we hunger for – because there is a yearning deep within us to want to discover, to understand, and to experience.

For better or for worse, we are influenced by the stories we hear, see, read, and share. That is why the Christian liturgy, rich in scripture and stories of faith, has a deeply formative power. Over time, as we encounter the presence of God in the liturgy, we become what we receive. As darkness settles each night and we prepare to rest for a new day, again and again we turn to stories – in our thoughts and in our dreams – to remind us of who we are, what we are, and where we should be going.

Stories have the power to shape us in ways that turn us toward the Good and away from the Bad. Unfortunately, the reverse is also true. It's a simple act, but a good story can have positive life-changing consequences – both to the individual and to the world. Sharing a story, whether by radio, TV, book, computer, or word-of-mouth, helps us understand ourselves, our world, and our proper relationship with God. This, then, is the **POWER OF THE STORY**.

THE ACTS OF PAUL AND THECLA

THE story of Paul and Thecla, and the beginnings of the Christian faith, was immensely popular among the young people in the first century AD. Thecla became a real folk hero, and eventually one of the most popular female saints of early Christianity.

Not everything that happened to Saint Paul on his missionary journeys to evangelize the Gentiles in Asia Minor and Greece was recorded in the book "The Acts of the Apostles" in the Bible New Testament. Ancient writers, historians, and scholars recorded many other interesting details that never made it into the Canon of Scripture. Even though not fully validated as factual, such worthy accounts, tales, and narratives that interpreted and expanded the Biblical account – to fill in the blanks between the lines, so to speak – often provided new insights and discoveries. What really happened to Paul on his journey? How did he inspire the people? How was he saved from the stone-throwing mob? Who were his friends and who were his enemies? Possible answers lie outside the text of the Bible in the ancient apocryphal writings.

The main story in this book roughly takes place in the time period 46-48 AD that is covered by the Biblical record between Acts 13:51 and Acts 14:21. This is the first missionary journey of Paul to spread the Good News of Christianity to the peoples outside of Judea and Samaria – to the ends of the earth (the Great Commission of Acts 1:8). It nearly ended in disaster. But, as we know, his epoch voyages of teaching and evangelization thankfully continued. And there is always that hidden desire to know what really happened – to fill in the blanks.

In this book, the people and places are real, and the dates are accurate – at least as accurate as the available ancient records indicate. But the story is fiction. Or is it? Maybe this is the way it actually played out. The story in this book is consistent with the Bible. But it is a story within the greatest story ever told – and it is a story worth telling. The emphasis here is not on the wizened and aged Paul, but on an intelligent and courageous 18-year-old girl. The story revolves around the rational thought processes that preceded her decisions and actions, and the consequences that resulted therefrom.

Whether myth or history, fact or fiction, one aspect remains – it's a darn good story – a 'tall-tale' like no other! So, what you read in this book is my contribution to the writings of the eminent ancient authors. I've tried to fill in the many gaps that people often find disconcerting, usually not by just inventing things from my imagination, but by researching the historical literature and then synthesizing a plausible story thread that, to me, is logically and syntactically sound. But, of course, the final review is up to the reader.

ALLEGORY

Mystery of the Mustard Seed [1]

Once upon a time, there was a tiny mustard seed – and he was sorely depressed. When he looked around at all the other seeds in the barn, he could see that they were all bigger, brighter, and beefier than he was. Compared to them, he was just a tiny ugly grain [2]– nothing but a minute speck of matter.[3] In fact, he was so insignificant, that all the other seeds paid him no attention. They busied themselves with embellishment and cosmetic enhancement for self-improvement and competitive advantage – often boasting that they were the biggest, the strongest, or the sweetest. As for the mustard seed, if they weren't laughing at him, they ignored him.

Sad and dejected, the mustard seed could often be heard moaning, "I am just worthless – the least of every seed that can be sown.[4] Just look at that giant wheat seed over there. He is huge compared to me, and has a beautiful rich reddish-brown nut-like color. And look at that sunflower seed, majestic in size and shape. O, woe is me! I am nothing – totally inconsequential compared to them. I am useless. No one will ever want me."[5]

One day, a local farmer, well known as a rustic sage, mystic, and philosopher, heard him lamenting about his lack of size and beauty. So, in a matter-of-fact manner, he said to the mustard seed, "Hey there – why so glum? It's not that bad, you know. Everything is really not what you think. You're just not seeing the big picture."

"How so?" said the mustard seed. "And I suppose that you do see the big picture?"

"Well, it just seems to me that you don't understand yourself at all," replied the farmer. "You're only looking at the outward appearance of yourself. But it is the inner appearance that is important. My friend, within you lies great potential. You see, there is a hidden image that exists inside of you – an image of a great and beautiful plant – and by the way, that plant can be miraculously created from the image![6]

"Really? An inner image?" retorted the mustard seed, somewhat sarcastically.

"Yes. It's true. There already exists an image inside of you that can transform into a live plant that will be 10 to 15 feet tall![7] No wheat plant ever grows that tall! And that plant can produce exquisite flowers and seedpods in great abundance, which can then produce many more plants – not to mention the benefit to birds and animals. So in truth, you are much more mighty than the wheat seed."

The little mustard seed heard what the farmer had said, and although he knew that the farmer had much experience in dealing with seeds of all kinds, he was in fact still a little skeptical. So, without beating around the bush, he asked the farmer straightforwardly, "Well, if that's true, how in the world do I get the image that's within me to reveal itself?"

To which the farmer replied, "It's pretty simple really. All that has to happen is that, by hook or by crook, you must be planted in the ground – and then you will start a transformation that will result in you becoming just like the image – you will end your existence as just a seed and start a new existence as a plant. The image within you will then come forth of itself."

"Yikes!", yipped the mustard seed. "All I have to do is be planted in the ground? What's up with that? You must be kidding – I don't want to travel to some strange place! I like it here in the seed bin in the barn! I just want to be recognized as a big, strong, and beautiful seed!"

"That's all fine and good," responded the farmer, "but the reality of it is that it just doesn't work that way for seeds. In fact, in all of nature there is not a single type of seed that can continue to exist in its present state, regardless of how big, strong, or beautiful it is, and still release the image that hides within it. You see, every seed has to be planted in the ground in order for him to be transformed into the image. That's just the way the designer designed it to work.

"Now, when that happens, you'll no longer exist as a mustard seed at all. No one will be able to recognize your jolly old mustard seed self, no matter how hard they try. You'll still exist, of course, but you will have been changed by a process of transformation – a process whereby you will be changed into something that looks just like the image that is inside of you."

Not wanting to fully embrace the farmer's explanation, the mustard seed hesitantly asked, "Isn't there any way that I can remain as I am and still have the image within me released?"

"Nope", said the farmer, "the transformation process won't even begin until you are planted in the ground. And there is something else you need to know – the transformation process doesn't happen overnight. There is a growth process involved that takes time. For the wheat seed, first the shoot appears, then the leaves, then the head (or spike) of flowers in the chaff hulls.[8] It's an ongoing process. Oh, and one more thing. You're going to have to die – even if you become big with beautiful flowers and create new seeds aplenty – you'll still have to die."

"Holy smokes! Now wait just a minute," interjected the mustard seed, "first you tell me that I need to be planted in the ground-ugh. Then you tell me that I have to endure a long growth process before I ever become that awesome image-ugh-ugh. And now you tell me that I'm going to have to die! Aargh – that's crazy! I don't want to die. I can live here in the seed bin forever.[9] If I'm going to have to pay the high price of dying in order for all of this to happen, then phooey! I want to become that image of a big plant with beautiful flowers right away, not off in the future! And I don't want to die!"

Considering the grumble of the mustard seed, the farmer inquisitively asked, "What 'high price' are you talking about? When I first heard you, you were complaining about how insignificant your life was as a seed. In fact, you were going on and on about how worthless you were, and how you so desired to be bigger and stronger.

"And then I come along, and tell you how you can exchange your trifling inconsequential existence for a tremendously exuberant and meaningful existence – and now, all of a sudden, you're placing a 'high price' on that same insignificant life that you were just complaining about before? So, which is it? You can't have your cake and eat it too, you know! Do you want to keep your humdrum meaningless life as it is, albeit for a long time perhaps – or do you want to change your life to something magnificent and purposeful, but only for a short time?"

The little mustard seed thought about that question for a time, and then responded, "Well, I'm not saying that I truly love my life as it is, but at least I'm very familiar with it. I know this life that I now have, and I know what to expect from day to day. What you're talking about sounds really appealing to me, but it's different and unfamiliar. I guess it's just that I'm afraid of the unknown – especially of change. What would that life really be like? If there are side effects that I don't like, can the process be reversed once it begins?"

"Sorry, no," said the farmer. "It can't be reversed. However, it can be aborted at any stage by the designer. Oops – forgot to mention that! For many seeds, the growth process is stopped at the shoot stage of transformation. Yes, they are changed from what they were before, but they are not like their image – not a big plant with beautiful flowers or fruit. They just remain at the shoot stage for the rest of their lives – it's surely less boring than their prior life as a seed. Then again, some seeds go on to the leaf stage, but then they remain there. At the leaf stage, there are just the tiniest hints of flower buds beginning to form, and they show great promise. But they just remain at the leaf stage for the rest of their lives – again, less boring than their prior life. So, I'm afraid that in only a very few seeds does the transformation process go on to completion, where they look just like the image that is within them."

The mustard seed then asked, "So, if I decide to be planted in the ground and start the transformation, and I accept the fact that the process is long and arduous, and I understand that I will eventually die, then why would any seed choose to do this if there was a good chance that the transformation process could be stopped and he would never get to realize the complete image? It seems to me that if you're willing to put up with the long process, and even to die as part of the process, then the risk of not achieving the full transformation into your image needs to be very small indeed. Otherwise, why would any seed want to be planted in the ground and start the transformation process? Better to live as nothing than to die without achieving anything."

"Well, good point. Right now, you are safe in my barn along with all of the other seeds, but once you begin this process and are taken outside and planted in the ground, there will be trials and tribulations. In the ground, you will be exposed to a new set of elements – wetness, dryness, temperature, pressure, and even disgorgement. There are risks. And once you germinate and reach the shoot stage, and then beyond, there are more risks. You'll be exposed to the elements of the weather that you've never really experienced before. You'll feel the scorching sun beating down on you. It's not always pleasant, but the truth is, you need the sun in order to grow. You'll feel the rain coming down on you. Sometimes it comes as a gentle shower and you'll enjoy that, but at other times it will come down in torrents – and the wind will be whipping you back and forth. The rain isn't always pleasant, but just like the sun, you need the rain to keep growing. And then there are the many predators, such as locusts, grasshoppers, and rodents, that will come and try to take your life away from you. They want to eat you so that they can continue to live and grow. You should be aware that only a small percentage of seeds that have started the transformation and have germinated to become plants, survive the entire growth process. Many just don't make it. They are lost to the elements or predators, and many just stop growing for reasons known only to the designer – it's all a great mystery, although I suspect it has something to do with the strength of the innate desires of the plant. So, that's it my friend, that's just the way it is."

The mustard seed gasped, "you mean that even if I was to begin this process, there is a good chance that I won't make it all the way to the end – to fully transform into my image and become a tall majestic plant with beautiful flowers and numerous seedpods – that I could just fizzle out and die along the way?"

"Yup – sad but true," replied the farmer. "It's just the way of life in general – how life was designed. Many plants don't survive. But here's the thing: it's important that you be planted in the ground in a good place. The ground you are sown in must be free of thorns and weeds, and must be fertile and not too rocky. It's possible that if there are thorn or weed seeds around, they will grow into plants so thick that they'll choke the life out of you, and you'll never sprout any flowers. And if the soil is too rocky or barren, your roots may not be able to get the nourishment that you need. These are big factors, but are out of your control – they're within the province of God only. But there is something that you can do to help maximize the chances of achieving that image. So, heed this advice my friend – first concentrate on putting down deep strong roots in the ground – otherwise, when the sun is scorching hot, you will wither – and when the ground is dry, you'll be able to reach water. It is the most important thing for you to do. You must concentrate on the roots, the part of you that can't be seen by others. Don't pay too much attention to what can be seen above ground, because if your roots are strong and healthy, the part of you that can be seen will then be strong and healthy also.

"As for why you, or any seed for that matter, would want to be planted in the ground and start the transformation process at all – well, I'm certain, my dear friend, that that desire has already been made for you by God, the designer and creator of everything. It is a great mystery. But if that desire was not already innate in you, then the whole life cycle process could unravel, and God's precious design could be unworkable. Whether you are ever planted in the ground, whether you ever germinate, whether you ever produce beautiful flowers and numerous seedpods, and whether any of your created seeds will undergo the transformation to realize their own image, are all ultimately in the hands and mercy of God. Sure, your health is important, and there is some luck involved. But whether you try your best or not, it's all up to God. He created your nature, and He knows it. So, the two of us here philosophizing about all this is intellectually interesting, but it really doesn't change anything. If you are planted, the transformation process will begin, and after that it's God's call."

Now the thoughts of the little mustard seed were conflicted. He really desired to become the fullness of his image – big, beautiful, and abundant flowers, with big, beautiful, and abundant seedpods, the seeds of which could be dropped back to the ground, or taken by other creatures, such that the seeds could then be re-dispersed back into the earth for eventual re-growth and re-harvest. But he was afraid of the pain and suffering that might come upon him – and he was fearful of the possibility that the whole growth process could be abruptly cut short, and he would never reach that awesome image – and experience its grandeur. And he was afraid of dying. But the farmer was right. He didn't really have a choice – he had to go for it. If he was ever planted in the ground, then he would start the transformation. And it was in his disposition – his nature – to try as hard as he could to achieve the fullness of the image. If God decided that it was not to be, then so be it. But he was going to try with all his might to become like the image. It was predestined for him to do so – that was his nature. He really had no free choice. And the final result was up to God.

Finally, after mulling all this over for a while, he had to ask the farmer a question: "I believe you when you say that I have this image inside me – and the potential for fully transforming into this image, although given the risks and possibilities involved, I may not make it – and the fact that I will eventually die. But I have one more question – a rather philosophical question that tugs at my soul:[10] Where exactly did my inner image come from, and why is the transformation process the way it is?"

Smiling assuredly, the farmer answered, saying, "Once again, it is a great mystery. But we do know that the design of all things, all processes, and all interrelationships, was completed by God, the all-knowing, all-powerful, and all-present (in time and space) creator of everything, before the earth was formed. The earth itself, and everything in it, represents the instantiation of that design.[11] And all organic things, living and non-living, follow the pattern of their designs. You are just following the pattern of your design.

"Now, at some point in the past, a pre-designed seed for a creature-being was fabricated and introduced onto the earth. The seed's name was Adam. He was the first seed in the earth that had an advanced image of God within him – not a perfect image, mind you – more advanced than any other, but still imperfect. Even you, my friendly mustard seed, have an image of God within you. It's just less advanced yet. You see, God looks like all things, and God is in all things. Because the image of God in each seed has been designed to be just right for that particular seed, each image is slightly different from the next. Even your next-door neighbor mustard seed has a slightly different image within him than you have.

"Now, like what will hopefully happen to you, the process of transformation into his inner image started for Adam. And he grew with the intention of realizing that image within him. However, unlike you my friend, the transformation process was not predestined. Adam was able to freely choose whether to stop the process, slow the process, or speed-up the process at every point along the way. This special ability was given to him by God and differentiated him from all the other creature-beings. He was a more complex life-form than an animal or a plant– he was a human being.[12]

"If he could have grown and matured to the extent where he fully reflected his inner image, then he would have been just like God – as would the seeds that he could create. And he would not die after creating those new seeds, but would continue to live forever in harmony with God.[13] But Adam couldn't reach his full potential – couldn't grow to fully reflect his image. Like every growing thing, he experienced trials and tribulations. And by free choice, his physical nature – his self-centeredness – overpowered his God nature – his God-centeredness – and he made choices that prevented him from fully realizing his image potential.[14] As a result, he lived a life of trouble and distress. He did manage to create new seeds, but eventually he died – and his created seeds were of a similar nature, and also died.

"Just like you will die, my friend. But if you start the transformation, grow enough, are mature enough, and are lucky enough, you can create new seeds. You can fully reflect your image and reach its full potential – your design allows for it – in that regard, you are blessed. But you cannot live forever – you are destined to die. There is no escape for you. On the other hand, the human beings like Adam, and myself, cannot fully reflect our image and reach its full potential. It's not in our nature – not in our design anymore – to be able to do so. Once it was, but now it's not. We will certainly die without becoming like our image. We can create more seeds, but they too are destined to die and never be able to fully reflect their image.

"Over time, the seeds resulting from Adam's seed became more and more self-centered.[15] They continued to make choices that stopped or slowed their transformation. Over generations, the image of God in them became weaker and even more unclear – until finally the image was almost gone.

"So, God the eternal designer and redeemer, out of pure love for His creation, fabricated and sowed a new seed. His name was Jesus Christ. He was the first seed in the earth that had the full perfect image of God inside Him. He was both fully God and fully human being. Unlike Adam, there was no doubt that He could transform into His image. Although He knew that He would suffer, and that the human part of Him would die, He nevertheless started the transformation, and vigorously grew with the full intention of realizing that image within Him. All of His choices along the way were right – He made no bad choices because His God-centeredness was greater than His self-centeredness. And the God part of Him did mature to fully reflect His image, but the human part of Him died in a passion of sacrifice. He sacrificed His human life so that all other human beings ever since could have the blessing of being able to continue to live forever in harmony with God, even though they can never fully reflect that image of God that is within them. He gave us the gift of grace.

"My little mustard seed friend, you are a plant and not a human being like me. But the basic processes are similar, as they are for the animal-creatures. You have an image of greatness within you. It can sustain you. But to bring that image to reality, the transformation must be started – existence as just a mustard seed must be ended – and the growth process to realize your potential as a full-grown mustard plant, mature with bountiful flowers and seedpods for dissemination, must be followed. Of course, it may not come to fruition, but the potential is there, and hopefully you will achieve it. I hope that you will be all that you can.

"The seeds of the animal-creature and the human being are slightly different than the plant in morphology and physiology, but the vital processes of biology are the same. We have a partial fuzzy image of God within us. You have the potential to realize the fullness of your image, but I do not. As for me, and all the other human beings, we were conceived when an egg cell united with a sperm cell and a fertilized seed was formed. The process of growth and transformation was immediate since, unlike plants, there is no dissemination of the seed – it is already nurtured inside the mother. When the seed sprouts – when we are born – we have already become the beneficiary of Jesus' sacrifice.[16] Although our growth process can be modified by choices we freely make – susceptible to our physical nature and self-centeredness, causing us to easily wither and fall away – we can still transform into the image that is within us. All we have to do is accept the sacrificial death of Jesus, with all of our heart and all of our mind, as the substitution of our own death. Then, we can be assured of transforming into the magnificent image of God that is within us. It's like the bounty of the big, beautiful, strong, and sweet fruit of an apple tree – or the abundant yellow flowers and hefty seedpods of the mustard plant. Our physical bodies will still die, but our spirit will be one with God. We can become just as the image within us. We can share eternal life with God in Heaven. It's our ultimate reward, but it's a new way of thinking and living – a new way of doing business for life on earth. We don't have to lose hope and give up on the transformation because the end result is unobtainable for whatever reason. We don't have to accept certain shortcoming. Nor do we have to overexert ourselves in a vain attempt to realize the image. We can be assured of realizing the image. We just have to accept the sacrifice of Jesus as a surrogate for our own life. If we do that with all of our heart, all of our soul, and all of our mind, then we are saved. We will complete the transformation and become the fullness of the image. What a wonderful gift that God has bestowed on all the creature-beings like myself – human beings.

"And so I ask all the other human beings out there: Are you willing to believe that Jesus Christ, fully God and fully man, willfully laid down his own earthly life, as a sacrificial stand-in for your own life, such that you could one-day be fully transformed into an image of God, and reap the eternal benefits of life in harmony with God? I hope that you are."

(Note: The concepts involved in this section were adapted from an original version by Gary Carpenter of Gary Carpenter Ministries, Tulsa, OK)[17]

ALLEGORY

NOTES

---

1. Matthew 13:31-32, Mark 4:30-32, and Luke 13:18-21 contain an account of Jesus' reciting of the 'Parable of the Mustard Seed' to his followers. The three features of the mustard plant emphasized by Jesus are the small size of the seed, the large size of the plant in relation to the seed, the rapid growth, and the robust reproduction. Popular analogies include 'Power of faith like a mustard seed' and 'Christ's kingdom to grow like a mustard seed'. The yellow flowering mustard plant grew wild in great abundance in ancient Palestine, and is considered by most people to be the source of the mustard seed mentioned in Scripture. There are wild mustard plants over 10 feet tall near the Jordan River even today. The stem of the plant becomes dry and wood-like, giving it the appearance of a tree (the mustard tree - Salvadora persica). However, this is not the source of the seeds used to make table-top condiment mustard today.

2. or kernel, or caryopsis

3. The mustard seed is the smallest seed of those which are 'planted in the ground' (but not the smallest seed overall). The seed does not need any cultivating, as it sprouts all by itself. There are few plants which grow as large in one season, and few plants that are characterized by such rapid germination of the seed. A seed planted one day could begin growing the next. With fleshy 1-1/2 to 3-inch leaves, the plant takes advantage of damp conditions near rivers and waterholes but can survive on fewer than 8 inches of rainfall per year.

4. Mustard is a member of the cruciferous vegetable family. It shares the same cancer-preventing benefits of broccoli, cabbage, and kale. It contains large amounts of beta carotene and vitamin C that are important antioxidants.

5. Seeds of the mustard plant provide widespread food for birds. In addition, when pressed, they yield an oil, present in amounts of 30-35%. The oil is edible but is used today mainly as an illuminant, for making soap and rubber substitutes, and in other industrial processes. There are ancient records that the mustard seed was used medicinally by Hippocrates. Note that a very different oil is obtained by grinding the seeds of the black mustard plant (a variant), and then treating it with water to cause a chemical action, resulting in a new oil not present in the tissues of the plant. This volatile, very irritating oil, was used to make the mustard gas weapon of World War I.

6. The pistil of a flower contains an ovary, within which are the ovules. A seed develops from an ovule. The 'image' referred to in this Allegory is the projected mature state of an embryo (or germ) that emerges from the zygote (newly fertilized egg cell) within the ovule after fertilization by pollination. The embryo is a miniature plant ready to develop into a mature plant given the right moisture, light, and thermal conditions.

7. From very small seedlings, the mustard plant grows rapidly and enters a phase of dense flowering - the blooms having an intense yellow color. The plants reach their full height as their flowers fade and after numerous green seedpods appear on their branches. The pods of brown mustard contain up to 20 seeds each, and those of white mustard contain up to 8 seeds. The plants are easy and inexpensive to grow; they flourish on many different types of soil, suffer from unusually few insect pests or plant diseases, and tolerate extremes of weather without serious harm. Flower buds are visible about 5 weeks after emergence. Yellow flowers begin to appear 7 to 10 days later and continue blooming with adequate water. About half of the flowers produce dark, reddish-brown seeds that are retained in pods of 0.5 to 0.75 in. in length. Flowers pollinated during the first 15 days of the flowering period produce most of the seed.

8. also called 'glumes'

9. Obviously, not forever. But the seed can exist in the seed bin a whole lot longer than the one-generation life cycle of the growing and mature plant. Some seeds can live hundreds of years under the right conditions.

10. All living things have a soul. The more complex the creature, the more complex (or advanced) the soul. The human being has the most complex soul, but also has a spirit given to it by God at conception. The spirit is the center of God consciousness, unavailable to all lower forms of life.

11. In engineering terms, the instantiation of a design is the process whereby the blueprint for an item (the design) is transformed into the physical item (the creation).

12. see Endnote 10; Adam was the first creature to have an advanced soul and a spirit.

13. or for a much longer time (determined by God) than would otherwise have resulted from 'the Fall'

14. Of course, this is the well-known Garden of Eden episode in Genesis, where Adam and Eve are tempted by the devil. Their self-centeredness overcame their God-centeredness, and they were prevented from achieving the fullness of their image (as were all of their descendants until the death and resurrection of Jesus Christ).

15. The essence of self-centeredness is called 'sin'. Although many other definitions of 'sin' exist, this is the basic tenet. Everything boils down to this.

16. We became the beneficiary of Jesus' sacrifice at conception, when we became identifiable as a 'person'.

17. Gary Carpenter Ministries, P.O. Box 9667, Tulsa, OK; Accessed Feb2020 at http://www.garycarpenter.org/.

1 FAITH ACCEPTED AND TESTED IN ICONIUM

"I am desperately in search of Paul, having been delivered from the flames"

THE YEAR is 48 AD.

THE PLACE is on the road between Antioch Pisidia[1] and the outskirts of Iconium,[2] in the region bordering the Roman provinces of Phrygia and Galatia, in central Anatolia.[3]

THE SETTING: It is the First Missionary Journey of Paul. Barnabas, John Mark, and Paul have sailed from Paphos in Cyprus to Perga in Pamphylia in Anatolia. Wishing to return to Jerusalem, John Mark departed and Paul and Barnabas then traveled north to Antioch Pisidia, where they addressed the people in the synagogue on the sabbath. But because of threatening accusations by influential Jewish leaders and sympathizers, Paul and Barnabas have left Antioch Pisidia, after preaching to the Jews the first week and to all the town residents the following week.

The question was the same one that had been asked every day this past week: "Father, are the teachers coming today?"

And the answer, of course, was the same. "I don't know, my son. Let's go to the signpost at the edge of the town and

19

wait. Hopefully, we can see them coming."

The young boy's name is Zeno. He is smart, eager, and craves learning about, and discovering new things. When he heard that special teachers were coming into town, he just had to be the first to listen to them and absorb everything they had to impart.

His father is named Onesiphorus,[4] a prominent merchant in an old Greek town that was now under Roman jurisdiction. He had heard about the life and ministry of a certain Jesus of Nazareth from traveling merchants, was sympathetic to the teachings, and wanted to learn more. When he received a letter from his old friend Titus, a teenage school buddy, that two disciples of the Jesus cult were coming to Iconium, he was very intrigued. He yearned to learn more about this new religion and was looking forward to meeting them. For both father and son, it was a fresh and exciting event.

ARRIVAL IN ICONIUM

MANY people, both Jew and Gentile, had listened to the teachings of Paul and Barnabas in Antioch, and many had become disciples. But many others had hardened their hearts in opposition, and resented their presence. Quickly, they formed a posse and confronted the two missionaries with an ugly ultimatum – "leave town or face the consequences." They could not accept a free and open dialogue. So, Paul and Barnabas decided to slip away quietly and travel to Iconium, a town slightly to the southeast. To help ensure their safe departure, two of the new 'disciples' decided to accompany the missionaries, since they were 'going that way anyway'. They were named Demas and Hermogenes.[5]

Although claiming to be believers and followers, Paul could sense that their hearts were conflicted. Nevertheless, he treated them with the same love, respect, and affection as all the other disciples he had come to know. During the long walk on the road, he explained to them all about the oracles and doctrines of Jesus, and the Good News of salvation and eternal life, just as it had been revealed to him on another road, on another fateful day.[6] But he couldn't help holding lingering doubts about their sincerity, and whether they might just be opportunists in disguise.[7]

Now, Onesiphorus had brought his family – his wife Lectra, and his sons Simmia and Zeno – to the crossroads at the outskirts of the town, where travelers from all directions would come to meet and greet residents and fellow traders alike. They hoped to be able to spot Paul and Barnabas, so as to meet and welcome them, and invite them to their house, although they had never actually seen them before.

Titus had given them a description of Paul's personage, both his appearance and his character, so they had an inkling of what to look for. They tirelessly stood by the edge of the road waiting with anticipation, comparing all who passed by with the description given them.

At length they saw a man coming of small stature, with balding head and ample beard. He was somewhat bow-legged, solidly built, and had greyish eyes, meeting eyebrows, large crooked nose, a mixture of pale and red in his complexion, and a sprinkling of grey on his head and beard – he fit the description. And he was full of presence. At one glance he would seem as a commoner, and at the next glance as a wizened philosopher. There was an air of dignity and wisdom about him. When they finally caught eye of each other, they immediately felt a connection – and they were joyful.

"Hail, servant of the blessed God," shouted Onesiphorus. To which Paul replied, "The grace of God, and our Lord Jesus Christ, be with you and your family." Then they warmly exchanged salutations and introductions to all.

But Demas and Hermogenes were moved with envy and jealousy. Under the pretense of equanimity, Demas said, "But are we not also servants of the blessed God? Why did you not salute us as such?"

With poise and composure, Onesiphorus replied, "Because I have not immediately perceived in you the fruits of righteousness, as I have in this man – my apology – please do not be offended – I may have been short-sighted. If you truly are of this disposition, then you shall be welcome in my house also." With that, they all followed Lectra and the boys back to their house, while Paul, Barnabas, and Onesiphorus chatted excitedly.

PAUL PREACHES THE GOOD NEWS

THERE was great joy among the family once back in the house, and with sincere hospitality they invited friends and neighbors over to help witness the wisdom and grace of the two missionaries. Together, they engaged in prayer, the breaking of bread,[8] and group discussion about their journey and experiences in Galilee, Samaria, and Judea.

At length, Paul began to earnestly preach the Word of God concerning a self-control lifestyle, humility, temperance, belief, salvation, and the resurrection. The room became quiet and everyone listened attentively to his words on God, life, and faith. The windows were open and passers-by could clearly hear Paul as he expounded upon points near and dear to his heart and his faith.[9] Many people that day heard and remembered his inspired and insightful message:

Blessed are the pure in heart, for they shall see God.

Blessed are they who keep their flesh pure and undefiled, for they shall become a temple of God.

Blessed are those who exercise temperance and self-control, for God will reveal himself to them.

Blessed are they that remain aloof from this world and forsake secular enjoyments, for they shall be called upright and righteous by God.

Blessed are they who have wives, and treat them not as property or slaves, for they shall receive favor from God.

Blessed are they who humbly accept the Word of God during times of trouble, for they shall receive consolation and become like angels of God.

Blessed are they who keep their baptism pure, for they shall find peace with the Father, Son, and Holy Spirit.

Blessed are the merciful, for they shall obtain mercy.

Blessed are they who pursue the wisdom and doctrine of Jesus Christ, for they shall be called the sons and daughters of the Most High.

Blessed are they who observe the commandments of God, for they shall dwell in eternal light.

Blessed are they, who for the love of Christ, abandon the riches and glories of this world, for they shall be judged as angels, placed at the right hand of the Father, and not suffer the bitterness of the final judgment.

Blessed are the bodies and souls of virgins, for they are acceptable to God and shall not lose the reward of their chastity, for the Word of our heavenly Father shall become the means to their salvation, and they shall enjoy life and rest forever.[10]

Whereupon, the house of Onesiphorus was blessed with joy and good will.

In the following two weeks, different acquaintances would come and go to the house now and then, and many strangers, out of curiosity, would gather outside the window to listen. Paul and Barnabas continued to preach the Good News almost every day in the same room to all who would listen, and many people were comforted.

BY THE WINDOW

KITTY-CORNER[11] across the town square was the house of the widow Theoclia, her 18-year-old daughter Thecla,[12] and two servant girls who lived with them. The husband and father had joined the Roman army, been shipped overseas, and never returned. The reports were that he had been killed heroically in battle, honorably serving the Emperor Claudius.[13] The family was among the 'first citizens of the Iconians' and well-off financially, but the lack of a male breadwinner resulted in some social difficulties and stigma.

Thecla had a bedroom facing the square, and when her window was open, she could often hear the chatter and verbal exchanges coming from the house of Onesiphorus. As it be, when his guest Paul began speaking on the evening of his arrival, Thecla happened to be by her window and could readily hear everything that he was saying. His words were appealing and rang true to her heart. And so, she listened attentively. Although she could not see his figure directly, she was fascinated by the eloquence of his discourse.

Once again the next day, she found herself by her window when Paul was speaking, and once again she was intrigued and enamored with his message. She noticed that many women, young and old, were going in to stand in the presence of Paul, and to hear his words of Good News. She earnestly wished that she could go also, but she was forbidden to leave the house unescorted. As the days went by, she made it a point to always be by her window when she thought Paul might be speaking. And little by little, she heard more and more, absorbed it all, and eventually became enraptured with his stories, philosophy, advice, and religious conviction. She especially took notice of his teachings on the one true God, and faith in Jesus Christ. But his teachings on chastity, temperance, purity, and self-control really hit close to her heart. She became mesmerized listening to Paul, and spent most of the day by her window, hoping not to miss a single word that he might say. For three days, she didn't eat, drink, or work – always glued to the window. But as such, she neglected her chores and activities – and at that her mother, along with the maids, became irritable.

Try as she might, Theoclia could not pry Thecla away from the window. Sweet words, harsh words, rewards, punishments – nothing worked. Thecla remained in deep contemplation staring out the window. At length, Theoclia decided to take more drastic measures – she would call on the young man who, by prior arrangement, was planned to become her husband. His name was Thamyris, and he was a prominent citizen of the town. Surely, he would be able to persuade her to return to normalcy and forget this strange babbling foreigner. So, she sent one of the servant girls to fetch him.

When Thamyris arrived, he asked, "So where is my dear Thecla?"

In reply, Theoclia said, "Thamyris, I have something very strange to tell you. For the space of three days now, Thecla will not move from her window – not so much as to eat or drink – but is resolutely intent on hearing the artful, divisive, and inappropriate discourses of a traveling foreigner. I am completely astonished at all this! How could a young woman of known modesty and reputation suffer herself to be so prevailed upon? In fact, that strange man has disturbed the whole city of Iconium, not just your Thecla. Many of the young men and women of the town flock to him – I've seen them – to listen to his odd doctrine. He tells them that there is only one God who alone is to be worshipped, that we should abandon all riches, and that we ought to live in chastity. And amazingly, my daughter Thecla, like a spider's web fastened to the window, is captivated by the discourses of this man they call Paul. She listens eagerly and attentively – and sincerely believes everything that he says. In this manner, I think the young woman has been seduced.

"Now, you must go and speak to her, for she is to be your future wife. Even now, she'll just be staring out the window. Be assertive and command her to stop this nonsense!"

Accordingly, Thamyris went to her room and greeted her with care, so as not to precipitate an angry response, saying "Thecla, my beloved, why are you sitting in this melancholy state for so long? What are you thinking? What strange things have you been listening to? What peculiar impressions have overpowered you? Please come back to me and tell me you will be yourself again."

But Thecla said nothing and turned not her head.

Her mother then pleaded with her, "My child, why do you make no reply – and sit so glum and gloomy like one intent on despondency?"

Again, Thecla said nothing and turned not her head.

After a period of silence that seemed like an eternity, Theoclia and Thamyris gave up their beseeching and sadly left the room. They didn't know what to do. Was Thecla to be lost to them? After moaning about the situation for a while, they began to say things outside her door (purposefully loud enough for her to hear) that they thought might dissuade her through embarrassment, fear, or some other logical persuasion. Even the maids chimed in with laments.

But none of this had any effect. Thecla was not even inclined to take notice of them, much less respond, for she was intent on contemplating the mighty words of Paul. She just couldn't take her mind off the power of his sermons.

Out of frustration, Thamyris ran into the square to observe just who were going in to the house to see this Paul, and what they were saying when they came out. There, he happened to come upon two strangers that were engaged in amicable argument just outside the house, and politely asked them, "Sirs, do you know the man in this house that preaches all the sermons? Do you have any business with him? I understand that he deludes the minds of young people, both boys and girls, persuading them not to marry, and to give up pursuits of wealth and happiness. Is this true? Are you believers in his doctrine?"

The two strangers were Demas and Hermogenes, taking a break in the cool evening air. "Yes, we know him. But we can't say anything about him," they replied, with a slight wink of the eye and nod of the head, intimating that for the right price, more information could be divulged.

"Well, I promise to give you a considerable sum of money if you will give me a just account of him, for I am a known respectable citizen of this city," countered Thamyris.

"We cannot say exactly who he is," continued Demas, "but we have traveled with him, and know that he deprives young men of their intended wives, and young women of their intended husbands – by teaching that even if you believe in his one god, you cannot be resurrected after death, unless you continue in chastity for the rest of your life, and do not defile your flesh."

Thamyris was now getting very concerned, and suspecting that they had not told him everything, said to them, "Please, won't you come along with me to my house now and partake of some drink and refreshment. Maybe you can tell me more about this Paul."

And so, the three of them went to the house of Thamyris.

BEFORE THE GOVERNOR

THEY arrived to a very splendid entertainment where

there was wine in abundance and very rich provision. They were brought to a richly spread table, and Thamyris encouraged them to drink plentifully. His goal, of course, was to get them to open up, so they would 'spill the beans' on Paul – tell him what he could use to have Paul extradited or arrested – such that Thecla would then return to him. Of course, it was less about any love he might have for Thecla – and more about possibly losing his stature in the community for not having the proper doting wife. In any case, it made him angry and jealous.

At the right moment, Thamyris said, "I would like to know more about these teachings of Paul – I really need to understand them. You see, I am concerned about my fiancée. She seems to delight in that stranger's discourses, and has withdrawn from me to such an extent that I am in danger of losing her."

Then Demas and Hermogenes together answered, "If you want to rid yourself of this man, you should have him brought before Governor Castellius – as one who endeavors to persuade the people into the strange new religion of the Christians – a religion that does not revere the gods of Rome. Then, by the order of Caesar, he will have the authority to put this man Paul to death – thereby releasing his hold on your fiancée. At the same time, we can teach her that the resurrection in which he speaks of, has actually already occurred. For when we have children, it is like being risen again and coming to the full knowledge of God."[14]

Thamyris then knew what he had to do. He rose early in the morning, gathered together some prominent officials and magistrates, a jailer, and a large number of townsfolk armed with sticks and clubs. They marched into the house of Onesiphorus, with Thamyris shouting: "The man here named Paul has deceived the citizens of Iconium with his false teachings, especially my fiancée, who will no longer look at me or speak to me. He is a false prophet, not honoring the gods of Caesar, and dangerous to the state – he is not wanted in this city. Therefore, he must go with us straightaway to see Governor Castellius." And the whole crowd cried out, "Away with this impostor, for he has perverted the minds of our wives, and all the people who pay attention to him."

Barnabas and Onesiphorus were no match for the frenzied crowd, and Paul was shepherded off to the governor's office in the courthouse. Once there, Thamyris stood before the governor's bench and spoke in a loud voice, "Honored Proconsul, I do not know where this man comes from, but he is one who teaches falsehoods and perversions. He teaches that matrimony is a hindrance to achieving a resurrection after death, and this makes our young women averse to marriage. This runs against the will of Caesar! Therefore, I ask you to command him to tell us why he teaches this nonsense."

Snickering, Demas and Hermogenes then whispered to Thamyris, "Tell him that he is a Christian, and he will be shortly given the sentence of death."

But the governor intervened before he could say anything and addressed Paul, saying "Who are you, and what do you teach? These reputable citizens bring grave accusations against you."

To which Paul responded, saying "Since I am now called to give an account of my teachings, honored Sir, I respect your audience. Let me tell you this: The one God, who is a God of love, but also of vengeance,[15] and who has need of nothing but the salvation of his creatures, has sent me to reclaim them from their wickedness, corruption, and uncleanness – from carnal pleasure, and even from death – and to persuade them to sin no more. For this reason, God sent to us his only Son Jesus Christ, about whom I preach, and in whom I instruct men to place their hopes. He alone has had compassion on a world led astray, such that people may no longer be under judgment of the Hebrew law, but may have faith in the ways of God, the knowledge of the Good News, and the love of truth. Therefore, if I teach things that have been directly revealed to me by God, where is my crime?"

When the governor heard this, he was taken aback, and unsure of what to do. So, he ordered Paul to be bound and put in prison until he had more time to think the whole thing through – and then to decide how to proceed with prudence. Barnabas protested, but Paul was led off to the prison and incarcerated in a jail cell.

IN THE PRISON

THAMYRIS returned to the house of Theoclia and told her quietly all that had happened, thinking their conversation was private. They were both relieved, and comforted each other with words of confidence that Thecla would 'return to normal' in a day or so. But unbeknown to them, Thecla heard what they had said. In her contemplative state, her senses had been sharpened. Like Thamyris, the day before, she knew what she had to do. She had to see Paul.

Shortly after midnight, Thecla dressed herself in plain, unassuming, working-class clothes, complete with hood to cover her face and hair. She put in her pocket some expensive pieces of jewelry – earrings, bracelets, anklets, and a silver mirror. Stealthily, she snuck out of the house and carefully made her way to the prison. The door was open, so she entered and addressed the prison guard in charge:

"I come to see the prisoner named Paul."

"Visiting hours are over," said the guard. "Go home and come back tomorrow."

Expecting such a response, Thecla flirtatiously hinted that if he let her in, she would respond with favor. The guard seemed amenable – after all, it was the middle of the night.

"If you let me in, I will give you these expensive bracelets."

"I don't know," hesitated the guard, "I was thinking more along the lines of …"

Cutting him off, Thecla then added, "And if you let me in right now, and say nothing about it to anyone, I will give you these opulent earrings. And maybe more when I come out. I won't be long."

With that, the guard let her in, and told her where Paul was being kept. But there was another snag. As she approached his room, there was a jailer sleeping in the nearby corner. He was in charge of this particular ward. She tried to slip by him on tiptoes, but he awakened.

"Who are you?" the jailer asked.

"I have been given special permission by the prison guard to visit Paul for a short time," replied Thecla. "I would be grateful if you let me into his room." With that, she flashed her silver mirror, implying that he could have it. The jailer, thinking she was a prostitute, agreeably took the mirror with satisfaction, let her in, and went back to sleep.

Paul was in personal prayer and surprised when she entered. He wasn't sure what to think when the attractive young woman removed her overcoat and stood before him.

"My name is Thecla," she blurted out. "I live on the square by the house of Onesiphorus. I have listened to your sermons from my window, and I am very joyful at hearing these teachings. I very much wish to be a disciple of yours – a Christian – and to learn everything that you can teach me."

"My dear child, you should be home with your family, safely in your bed," muttered Paul. "This is no place for you."

"I'm afraid that I may never see or hear you again. You have given me hope and a new look on life. I can't bear the thought of not having met you, and not learning everything I can from you."

"But your family ...," interjected Paul.

"My mother wants to marry me off to a prominent citizen, but I do not love him, and do not wish to be married to him. We are not compatible – we don't have similar ways of thinking. I would not be happy spending my life with him. Instead, I want to fulfill my own desires and seek my own destiny. I want to follow you. I want to live like the Christians who follow you. My mother and fiancé do not like Christians. They think you are like magicians and sorcerers – and atheists, because you don't worship the gods of Rome.[16] I can't live there anymore. Please do not throw me out. I want to learn everything about the Christians. Please teach me. I beg you to teach me everything about your religion, so I can follow it with all my heart, and urge others to do likewise."

Paul could sense the sincerity in her heart. And although he was tired and worried about the next day, he knew that he had to administer to her. So upon invitation, Thecla sat down on the dirty ground, and Paul related to her the whole story of Jesus the Christ, his birth, death, and resurrection, his own conversion, the Apostles in Jerusalem, and his mission to bring the Good News to the Gentiles throughout the world. They talked for hours, well into the morning light. The jailer and prison guard had forgotten about her, thinking she was just another floozy.

Thecla had great admiration for Paul. She perceived him to be a man of courage, who was unafraid of suffering. At length, she said, "I am so happy that you have told me all this. You are truly a man given divine assistance. I want to follow your path and be a Christian." And then, in humble appreciation, she kissed the chains that bound him.

BACK BEFORE THE GOVERNOR

By mid-morning, the family had realized that Thecla was missing. Theoclia, Thamyris, and the maids searched all over the town, but could not find her. Finally, one of the workers at the nearby inn said that he saw her talking to the night porter last night. So, they found the night porter at his home, woke him up, and asked him about it. When questioned, he told them that she had asked him for directions to the prison. "I told her to go home – that she shouldn't be out this late at night, but she persisted. So, I showed her the way to go, and she went off speedily."

Following the porter's directions, Theoclia and Thamyris then made straight for the prison. They surmised that she had gone to see Paul. When they arrived at the jail cell, sure enough – there were Thecla and Paul, both asleep on the ground. Shocked beyond words, they told the morning jailer to keep watch while they went to enlist the help of the governor. They gathered some townsfolk together, went to the governor's office, and told him everything that had happened.

The governor then ordered Paul to be brought before the bench at the courthouse. Forthwith, he was awakened, dragged from the cell, and brought before the governor. The townsfolk shouted angrily, "He is a magician and disrespects the gods. Let him be put to death!"

Unperturbed by the noisy throng of commoners, the governor asked Paul what had happened – and Paul gave him the whole story of how Thecla had come to him seeking knowledge and truth, and how the night was spent in teaching her the gospel of history – the holy works of Jesus, the Christ.

The governor then ordered Thecla to be brought before the bench. Aware that Paul had been taken, she was found moping on the ground in the cell, sulking and brooding, but defiant still. Heeding the summons, however, she was willingly brought before the bench. By this time, a council of elders had arrived.

With everyone in place, the governor asked Thecla directly, "Why will you not marry citizen Thamyris, according to the law of the Iconians?"

Thecla gave no answer, but looked pleadingly across the room at Paul, her eyes fixed upon his countenance.

Paul nodded and smiled assuredly, but was not at liberty to say anything – interfering in family matters was dangerous business.

After a few moments of silence, Theoclia could stand no more. Exasperated and at her wits end, she cried out, "Let the unjust creature be burned – let her be burned at the stake in the midst of the amphitheatre – as a lesson and warning for all young women – for refusing to follow the mores of our society, and for listening to the ungodly teachings of evil foreigners. Let them see the consequences and be afraid!"[17]

Astounded by this, the governor knew that he had to take action. The family of Theoclia had a well-known and respected name. Failure to heed her wishes could have political repercussions. Accordingly, he ordered that Paul be whipped and expelled from the city. Realizing that Theoclia was serious, he ordered that Thecla be brought to the amphitheatre straightaway for punishment. As for the severity of it, he hoped that either Thecla or Theoclia would have regret and pull-back, thereby avoiding a public spectacle, in spite of the public hunger for such exhibitions. And so, by order of the governor, Paul and Thecla were separated and each escorted out of the courtroom per their respective sentences.

ESCAPE TO THE CAVE

PAUL and Barnabas have been banished from Iconium. They have sought shelter in a small cave just outside of town on the road to Daphne.[18] Onesiphorus, his wife, and his two sons went with them, for moral support and a sign of solidarity. They were shuffled off in a hurry, with no time to pack any food or drink. Demas and Hermogenes did not come. And none of the other new believers, converts, or disciples joined them.

They fasted and prayed for several days – prayed for the citizens of Antioch and Iconium, and for Thecla, the young girl, full of faith and hope, who risked her life to visit Paul in prison and learn the Good News.

On the third day, the children said to Paul, "Sir, we are hungry and have nothing with which to buy bread."

Taking off his coat and giving it to Zeno, the oldest boy, Paul said to him, "Go back into town, my child, and buy some bread for us all, and bring it back here. There is money in the pocket."

And so, Zeno made his way back into town, went to the bakery in the square, and bought five loaves of bread with the money Paul had given him. As he was leaving the shop and crossing the square, he saw Thecla, his neighbor, wandering aimlessly about as if not knowing where to go or what to do.

Surprised, he called to her, "Thecla, where are you going? Are you OK?"

She answered excitedly, "I am OK. I am desperately in search of Paul, having been delivered from the flames."

Then the boy said, "I am going there now with this bread. I will take you to him, for he is very concerned about your welfare, and has been in prayer and fasting for three days now." Thecla was overjoyed that she had found the boy, and the two of them hurriedly ran back to the cave.

When they came to the cave, they found Paul on his knees praying aloud, "O Lord Jesus Christ, grant that the fire may not touch Thecla – but be her helper, for she is your faithful servant."

Then quietly coming up and standing behind him, Thecla cried out, "O sovereign Lord, Creator of heaven and earth, the Father of your beloved and holy Son, I give praise to you for having preserved me from the fire, and for being able to see Paul again."

Startled, Paul arose, turned around, and saw her standing right behind him. With great relief and thanks, he prayed in a loud voice, "O God, who searches the heart, Father of my Lord Jesus Christ, I give all praise to you for having answered my prayer."

Having heard Paul's voice and prayer, the others came running up from further back in the cave, where it was warmer. They saw Paul and Thecla in an embrace of happiness, and they were all filled with great joy and relief. Then, they prayed together and worshipped God for the good fortune. They now had five loaves of bread, with some herbs and water, so they shared a blessed meal while they solaced each other and reflected upon the holy works of Christ.

After a time, Barnabas asked Thecla what had happened to her in Iconium after separating from Paul and leaving the magistrate's courtroom. Paul, and all the others were curious as well. So, Thecla began to relate the whole series of events that happened to her in the amphitheatre.

IN THE AMPHITHEATRE

"GOVERNOR Castellius was exceedingly agitated," said Thecla. "He arose immediately and commanded all the elders, court staff, and interested onlookers to immediately report to the amphitheatre. When only he and I, and my mother and Thamyris, were left present, he pleaded for one of us to recant. When there was nothing but silence, he threw up his hands and pronounced judgment.

"Then, I was led into the wings of the theatre where participants made preparation. A bunch of young men and women were ordered to gather wood, straw, and hay. I saw some workers fumbling with a large post, and then I started to become nervous. I tried to run away but the guards held me tight. Soon, I heard the sound of people's voices coming from out in the arena, so I knew that something big was going on out there.

"But I kept thinking about all the messages that Paul had taught in his sermons – how we need to have faith in the one true God, and in His Son Jesus Christ, even during times of stress and adversity – and how we need to keep our minds and bodies pure in preparation for the resurrection. I knew that what Paul had said was right and that all these people were confused. I just couldn't go back to my earlier life, no matter what. So I said nothing.

"A short while later, an official barked something and two rough looking characters greedily came up to me and said, 'It's time.' With that, they loosely bound my wrists and then eagerly ripped off all my clothes until I was completely naked. Smirking, snickering, and making snide remarks the whole time, they then moved me to the entrance to the arena. Two policemen were waiting at the door.

"I was then escorted out to the center where a large stake had been erected, with dry wood arranged around it. They forced me to go up on the pile and stood me by the stake. Just before they lashed my hands behind it, I made the sign of the Christian cross, and yelled out, 'My God, forgive them.

They know not what they do.'[19] I remember the crowd was very noisy – most seemed to be cheering loudly.

"The governor himself came right up to me and said, in a soft voice, something like, 'What a shame. What a beautiful body you have. What a waste.' I thought I detected a tear in his eye. But he was only seeing the physical and not the spiritual. And then he exclaimed in a loud voice, 'Let it proceed!'

"Frantically, I looked around the multitude – as a lamb in the wilderness looks everywhere to find its shepherd – looking for Paul, or maybe supporters or friends. But all I could see were mad, angry faces.

"Then, suddenly, I saw the Lord Jesus Christ sitting among the throng. Our eyes met, but His face was in the likeness of Paul! My heart leaped for joy, and I said to myself, *Paul has come to be with me in my hour of need – praise the Lord.* But then, as I gazed upon him with heartfelt peace and sincerity, he morphed into a ghostlike image, and rose up into heaven in a swirling misty column. I wasn't sure what it all meant, but I knew that I was not alone. The Lord was with me."

THE SPECTACOL [20]

"**AND** then, to a great roar of the crowd, the workers set fire to the pile. I prayed to God with all my heart.

"And although a great fire was soon blazing, it did not touch me. For almighty God, having compassion upon me, caused a great trembling in the earth, followed by thunder, lightning, and buckets of rain and hail falling from the sky. The trembling and deluge covered the entire amphitheatre, and was so great that the support structures started to collapse and many in the crowd were injured and in danger of death. But thanks to God, nobody died, the fire was put out, and I was saved.

"There was terrible confusion and panic in the theatre, with people running in every direction. Amidst the chaos, the governor officially put a halt to the proceedings and ordered that I be given back my clothes and released. 'I bow down to the god of Thecla,' he stammered. 'Her god is truly powerful. I dare not cross her god.' Of course, despite everything Paul had said, he had no appreciation for the one true God.[21]

"After quickly dressing, and making my way out of the amphitheatre, I ran back to my house to look for my mother. But she was nowhere to be found – and neither was Thamyris. So I ran over to the house of Onesiphorus, but it also was empty. I spent the next two days wandering around looking for Paul, and for my mother. I didn't know what to do or where to go. And then, by the grace of God, I met up with Zeno, and together we ran here to the cave."

DEPARTURE TO ANTIOCH

"A remarkable story and a blessed outcome," said Paul.

"It was a miracle," added Barnabas.

Everyone was very thankful and relieved that she was safe – and they rejoiced in the glory and mercy of Jesus Christ until late in the day.

At length, Thecla said to Paul, "Sir, if you consent to allow it, I will follow you as a disciple wherever you go. I will cut my hair and change my wardrobe, if need be."[22]

He replied to her, "My dear Thecla: people are now much given to sin, vice, and fornication; and you being young and beautiful, I am afraid that you might meet with excessive and forceful advances, solicitations, demands, and even temptation. I worry that you might not be able to cope with it; to withstand it all – you could be overcome, either unwillingly or willingly."

But Thecla answered saying, "Grant me only the seal of Christ. Baptize me, and no temptation shall affect me."

Smiling gracefully, Paul rejoined, "Thecla, my dear friend and fellow believer, you must be patient. Continue to believe with all of your heart and all of your mind – and you will soon receive the baptism with water as a gift from Christ.

"You may accompany Barnabas and I if you wish – we are going back to Antioch. Onesiphorus, and his family, will return to their home in Iconium – we wish them well and bid them thanks for their support and hospitality."

And so, the next day, the group of believers left the cave, separated, and went their respective ways.

NOTES

---

1. Antioch Pisidia is not to be confused with Syrian Antioch, a place often visited by Paul and the early Christians, and one of the most important Roman cities in the eastern Mediterranean. Syrian Antioch is now a major town of southeastern Turkey, lying about 12 miles northwest of the Syrian border. It was once called 'the cradle of Christianity' as a result of its longevity, and the pivotal role that it played in the emergence of early Christianity. The New Testament asserts that the name 'Christian' first emerged there (Acts 11:26). Antioch Pisidia (also known as Antioch Phrygia), on the other hand, is in the Lakes Region of central Turkey, and is now basically just ruins. However, in the first century, it was a trading crossroad and may have accommodated a population of 100,000.

2. One of Turkey's oldest continuously inhabited cities, the Iconium of Roman times is known as Konya in the present day. As the capital of the Seljuk Turks from the 12th to the 13th centuries, it ranked as one of the great cultural centers of Turkey. During that period, the mystic Mevlana sect founded a Sufi order known in the West as the Whirling Dervishes.

3. Anatolia is also known as Asia Minor, the westernmost protrusion of the Asian continent, making up the majority of modern-day Turkey. The newly founded churches in Galatia were the target of Paul's letter to the Galatians (Epistle to the Galatians in the New Testament). Originally thought to have been written on his 2nd missionary journey (and visited again on his 3rd), many scholars now believe that it was actually written near the end of the 1st missionary journey.

4. Latinized form of the Greek name Onesiforos, which means 'bringing advantage to; profit-bearing/bringing; beneficial'

5. Hermogenes was a coppersmith by trade, but had fallen on hard times.

6. Acts 9:3-8

7. Both of Paul's traveling companions, Demas and Hermogenes, eventually renounce him and desert him (2 Timothy 4:10 and 1:15).

8. At this time, it was a custom that loaves of bread that had been prayed over, be broken for distribution to the faithful. This was a sign that all, even though many, were one loaf, one bread, and one body in Jesus Christ. The name eventually given to the Catholic Mass, came from the rite of breaking bread.

9. The house of Onesiphorus was in the town center. One wall of the house directly faced the town square. The living room wherein the guests were hosted was adjacent to that wall. And in the living room, there was a large window that looked out at the town square.

10. Compare with the blessings proclaimed by Jesus at the beginning of his 'Sermon on the Mount', known as the 'Beatitudes' (Matthew 5:3-12). Paul has added his own personal twists and slants to the story that had been told to him by the Apostles in Jerusalem.

11. The term 'kitty-corner' has nothing to do with cats. Instead, it stems from the expression 'cater-corner', which is derived from 'quatre', the French word for 'four'. It usually means a position diagonally across from another – in this case, a house diagonally across the town square.

12. The name 'Thecla' is of Greek derivation and means 'God's glory'.

13. Claudius served as Emperor ('Caesar') of Rome from 41 to 54 AD. He succeeded the depraved Caligula, and was succeeded himself by the ruthless and infamous Nero. At the beginning of his reign he treated the Jews with favor – he even restored all former rights and holdings to the Jews of Alexandria that had been earlier taken from them. But later his attitude changed, and he banished all Jews from Rome.

14. In 2 Timothy 2:17-18, two followers named Hymenaeus and Philetus, are impugned by Paul for having proclaimed that the resurrection had already taken place. This flawed way of thinking was widespread among followers who had fallen under the spell of false teachers.

15. or "is a jealous God"

16. Although the Christians considered the Romans to be pagans, the Romans considered the Christians to be atheists, because they didn't believe in and worship the Roman gods. Many Christians tried to explain to Roman authorities that they did worship a god, just not a Roman god that one could see a statue of. The attempt usually met with little success, especially when a 'Son of God' personage was introduced.

17. Theoclia wanted her daughter to be married in order to solidify the standing of her house in the community. With no marriage, she was afraid that their financial position would collapse (since there was no head male) and they would be reduced to 'commoners'. An unmarried daughter was a useless burden in her mind. Better to be rid of her in a fashion that elevated her own standing.

18. A small village not far from Iconium

19. This, of course, is analogous to Jesus' renowned saying while on the cross. Reference Luke 23:34.

20. This is a Romanian word, derived from the Latin, meaning 'spectacular show'.

21. Governor Castellius perceived that the god of Thecla was just another god within the greater pantheon of gods – albeit one that he had not yet heard of.

22. Thecla's thinking here is that she might be more readily accepted by society, and by the Christian community, if she looked like a man.

2 FAITH CHALLENGED AND FORTIFIED IN ANTIOCH

"In the Name of the Father, and of the Son, and of the Holy Spirit, I am baptized on this last day of my life"

THE PLACE is on the road between Iconium and Antioch Pisidia, in the region bordering the Roman provinces of Phrygia and Galatia, in central Anatolia.

THE SETTING: Because of expulsion by the Governor of Iconium, Paul, Barnabas, and Thecla have left the cave on the outskirts of Iconium and headed back to Antioch to comfort the believers, and to try once again to reach the non-believers.

ON THE ROAD TO ANTIOCH

PAUL, Barnabas, and Thecla have just arrived at the edge of the city when they are met and confronted by a group of men led by a prominent judicial officer named Alexander.

"You two fellows are the ones that caused disruption in our city a few days ago. We have been on the lookout for you, thinking that you might return. And you are the one called Paul," he said, pointing his finger and raising his nose and tone of voice. "You are not welcome here. You should leave."

"We only wish to comfort our friends," said Barnabas.

"If you do not leave now, you will be arrested, beaten, and

only the gods know what else." Then his voice became calmer. "But who is this lovely companion of yours? Does she belong to you? She was not with you when you were here last. She is like a breath of fresh air. Maybe she would like to be my guest and tour the city," smiled Alexander as he nudged closer to Thecla.

"She is not a relative of mine, but a friend, fellow believer, and traveling companion. And I don't think that she would want to be your guest in the city," replied Paul.

"Why don't we let her decide that," snapped Alexander. "I find her extremely coming, and find myself drawn to her even ever closer." He then moved very close to Thecla, finally grasping her by the arm, pressing his cheek to her cheek, and whispering something in her ear.

With that, Thecla had had enough. Swiftly and forcefully, she grabbed his overcoat and ripped it open. At the same time, she bashed his fancy royal hat and knocked it on the ground.[1] Looking about for help from Paul, she cried out in a distressed loud tone, "Don't touch me! Remove yourself from my presence! Although a stranger to you, I am a servant of the Most High God; and I am a principal person of Iconium."

But Paul and Barnabas were seized and held by companions of Alexander and could offer no assistance. Looking ridiculous in front of his friends, Alexander was incensed. With help from a friend, he grabbed her hands and tied them together with his scarf. "You will pay for that!" he exclaimed. "You will come with me to see the governor. Either you will be mine or you will be cast to the beasts!"

Paul started to say something, but was immediately cut off. "And as for you two," continued Alexander, "consider it a fair exchange. You are lucky we don't have you arrested. Leave now and you will not be harmed or indicted. But the girl comes with me."

Paul started to protest, but was quickly interrupted. "My patience and leniency wear thin. Leave now!"

With that, Thecla was forcefully escorted away while Paul and Barnabas were obliged to slink back down the road towards Iconium. Once out of sight of the unruly gang, Paul and Barnabas paused to reflect on what they should do next.

"We can't hope to rescue Thecla," said Barnabas. "It's just too dangerous. We'll be spotted for sure and arrested – or stoned – or worse."

"I'm afraid you're right. I wish we could do something, but I can't imagine any way to get her," reacted Paul. "We'll just have to pray to God every day for her safety. We have to put our faith in the Lord that He will see her through."

"But where should we go? Antioch and Iconium are both too dangerous now. Should we backtrack down to the sea?"

"No. I think we should continue to go east – to Lystra, which is just south of Iconium.[2] We cannot give up in despair. We must keep pushing forward – we must spread the faith as far as we can, as best as we can. Yes, to Lystra we should go. It's not too far."

Barnabas wasn't entirely convinced – they were getting a lot of hostile reaction from Jews and Gentiles alike, and their lives were constantly in jeopardy – perhaps a retreat to a more friendly region would be wiser. But Paul insisted, and he finally relented and agreed.

And so, with heavy heart, the two headed off to bring the Gospel to the people of Lystra.

IN THE HOUSE OF TIMOTHY

ARRIVING in Lystra, Paul and Barnabas headed to the town square (since there was no synagogue in Lystra), where they met a smart and open-minded man named Timothy.[3] After listening to Paul preach on the Good News, Timothy invited them to stay in his house, where they continued friendly discussions long into the night.

Paul and Barnabas continued to preach and evangelize near the house of Timothy for another three days. Many friends and neighbors came to listen, but few were converted.

Then, on the seventh day, as they were preaching in the town square, a group of seven or eight young people, dressed rather shabbily, approached them. Paul was apprehensive, thinking, *O my, this doesn't look good. What fresh persecution is now about to befall us?* One of the group headed straight for Paul, and standing next to him, pulled the hood from her head, and exclaimed, "I stand by Paul, great teacher of the Good News, loyal servant of the Most High God, and speaker of Truth. Who stands with me?"

It was Thecla! And all the people in the group stood by her and Paul in accord. She was dressed in the clothing of a man, wore no jewelry, and had her hair cut very short. She seemed to be in complete control and authority.

Paul was surprised and astounded that she had been able to get away, to find him, and make her way to where he was. "O my God, Father of my Lord Jesus Christ, it is you Thecla!" he shouted exuberantly. "You are alive and safe! I am so happy! Thank you Lord, for having answered my prayers. I feared the worst, but never gave up hope. God is truly on your side!"

Thecla answered saying, "O sovereign Lord, Creator of heaven and earth, I give you praise for allowing me to see Paul again."

Paul, Thecla, and Barnabas were all very happy and comforted each other, as well as the others in the group. They continued to rejoice and praise God until evening. Then, they all went back to the house of Timothy for rest and further reflection.

After a time, Paul remarked, "My dear friend Thecla, you have changed your outward appearance, but has your inner self changed also?"

To which she replied, "O Paul, my teacher and guide, I am the same person as you saw last week, and by the grace of God, I have been baptized in His name."

"But how did …?" Paul started to ask.

Anticipating his question, Thecla interrupted: "For the same Almighty God who assists you in preaching the message of Christ, has assisted me in surviving the trials of persecution and has allowed me to be baptized."

Of course, they all wanted to know more. In fact, they wanted to know everything that had happened to her after being forcibly abducted by Alexander and led away. So, Thecla began to relate the amazing story of her ordeals in Antioch – and how her faith was tested.

BEFORE THE PROCONSUL

"**ALEXANDER** and his friends conducted me into the city center with curses and foul-tongued blasphemies, all the while pushing, slapping, and striking me where they could. I did my best to fight them off – luckily, once we entered the residential area, they discontinued the physical abuse – but not the verbal. I didn't know where they were taking me but I feared the worst.

"Once within earshot of other reputable citizens, I shouted loudly, 'Help! Help me! A crime has been committed against me and I demand to see the governor.' I did this because I knew that the proconsul would have to shelter me until the sentence was enacted. I knew that I would be found guilty but this would buy me some time. If left in the hands of Alexander and his gang, I was afraid that they would beat me, rape me, or kill me that very night. Being 'upstanding'

THE PASSION OF THECLA

citizens, and the fact that some 10-15 people were concerned
and willing to go with us to the governor's office, the gang
had no choice but to follow on.

"We all went straightaway to the city court-house, where
the governor asked what happened. Of course, the men gave
a one-sided account that made me look like the aggressor, and
of course, being a stranger, a woman, and an unaccompanied
traveler, I wasn't even given the opportunity to rebut or give
my account. And of course, I was found guilty of assault.
Burning some incense, the governor entreated me to repent
and pray to the gods for mercy. But I refused, saying 'There
is only one God and His Son my Lord Jesus Christ, in whose
name I put my faith.' With this, the governor smirked and
then asked Alexander what he thought the punishment
should be – to which he replied, 'Her assault was a sacrilege
against my body, which is favored by the gods. For this
unacceptable crime, she should be thrown to the beasts! She
deserves no better!' In actuality, he was just very angry that
he couldn't have his way with me, and given this, that I should
be executed like a common criminal.

"Many of the gathered citizens were irritated at the
suggested decision. Some of them shouted, 'Shame! This
judgment is unfair, overly harsh, and evil! Shame! Shame on
the court if this be the final decision!'. But it was all to no
avail. Alexander was a 'reputable' citizen and I was a stranger
– a nobody. The proconsul issued the verdict and the
sentence: 'The woman is found guilty. She will be thrown into
the arena, and cast to the beasts! It shall be so!'

"The citizens continued to protest the unjust judgment,
but it didn't matter – it was too late. Alexander was ordered
to organize the spectacle. The governor then asked, 'Is there
anyone here who will lodge this woman for the next few
nights?'

"Whereupon, one of the outspoken citizens, a certain

wealthy and respected widow named Tryphina – a relative of the Emperor – spoke up saying, 'I will take her in, and give her food and shelter, as if she were one of my own family.' The governor agreed, and I was released in the custody of Tryphina, and ordered to report the next day to the amphitheatre for preparations."[4]

"As it turns out, Tryphina's only child, Falconilla, had only recently died, and she was still in grieving. And so, she began to treat me in her house as if I was a replacement for her own daughter. She was extremely kind and attentive – and very empathetic when I told her of all my troubles in Iconium."

TO THE AMPHITHEATRE

"THE next day, we had to go to the amphitheatre for familiarization and exhibition with the wild animals. I was cut, bled, and brought before them, so they could sniff my odor and know that I was a danger to them. The organizers do this to get the animals riled up against their intended victims. I was put into a den with an exceedingly fierce lioness, separated from it by only a partially slotted gate. I could see the lioness and it could see me and smell me. At first I was afraid, but I just thought about God and Jesus; and then the lioness became gentle, laid down in front of me, and licked my feet through the gate.

"Tryphina was with me, and when she saw this she grieved, 'O God, the judgments of this city are so terrible – unfair and unrighteous.' The onlookers were astonished, but the workers were unconcerned – they were just doing their jobs. After 'showing' me to the beasts, I was allowed to go home, but told that I would be summoned the next day."

"Early the next morning, Tryphina came to me troubled,

and said 'Thecla my child, my dear departed daughter Falconilla has come to me in a dream. She begged that I treat you as my own daughter in her place – she even called your name – the 'forsaken Thecla'. She asked me to ask you if you could intervene with your God on her behalf, such that she might be translated to a state of happiness and eternal life in a higher heaven.[5] Can you pray to your God for this? Can you teach me how?'

'O Thecla, I am so pained because we must go to the theatre again today. I'm afraid that I may lose you as I once lost my Falconilla. It is too much to bear! I have prayed to the gods but they don't seem to listen. Thecla, I sense that the God you follow is very strong. Please teach me how to pray to Him.'

"When I heard this, I was emotionally moved, and prayed to God saying: 'O Lord God of heaven and earth, Jesus Christ, Son of the Most High, please grant my request that Falconilla receive eternal rest and happiness with You, now and forever.[6] Amen.' Upon hearing this, Tryphina sighed again and groaned, 'O unrighteous judgments! O unreasonable wickedness! It is not right that such a beautiful creature should again be cast to the beasts!' "

"Within the hour, there was a sharp knock on the door, followed by the voice of Alexander shouting, 'Bring the criminal forth – the governor and the people are waiting. The proconsul has taken his seat, and the crowd is clamoring. I will take her now to fight with the wild beasts.'

"But Tryphina ran at him, shouting, pushing, and flailing her arms. 'Get out, you evil heathen, go away, leave us!' she screamed. Alexander backed off but was unconcerned. The henchmen from the governor's office were just a few paces behind.

"The soldiers arrived shortly and I was forced to

accompany them to the amphitheatre. Tryphina wept sadly, 'A second mourning has now come upon my house, and there is no one able to relieve me – either for the loss of my daughter, or for being unable to save my guest. O God of Thecla, I pray that You help her; she is Your humble servant.'

"Tryphina held me by the hand all the way to the theatre, murmuring 'O woe is me! I went with Falconilla to her grave, and now I must go with Thecla to the beasts.'

"When I heard this, I prayed weeping, 'O Lord God – in whom I have put my trust, who delivered me from the fire, and to whom I have fled for refuge – please reward Tryphina for her compassion to me, and for her help in preserving my chastity and well-being.'

"Upon arrival and entering through the doors of the arena, there was a tumultuous rumble from the gathered crowd of spectators, a mighty roar from the assembled beasts, and a cry from the people, 'Bring in the criminal! Away with the sacrilegious one!'

"But others clamored,[7] 'Shame! Shame! The city is irresponsible for this vile action! The cruelty is unwarranted and reprehensible – O horrible sight – O unrighteous judgment!'

"And Tryphina cried out, 'Let the whole city suffer for this crime! Order all of us, O governor, to be given the same punishment!' "

IN THE ARENA

"**TRYPHINA** was then forcibly taken away and I was moved to a makeshift shack at the edge of the field area. Here, I was stripped naked and given a simple waist-cloth to wear.[8] Then, I was shuffled out to the center of the arena, and wild lions and bears were let loose.

"Now, the lioness that had bonded with me the day

before, immediately came running to me – and the crowd screamed – but she submissively lay down at my feet. She would be my protector. A few minutes later, a fierce bear came running toward me with intent to attack – and the crowd screamed again. But my lioness protector intercepted the bear and tore it to pieces.

"Then there came a mighty male lion, ferocious and savage. It belonged to Alexander, and had been trained expressly to attack people. He wanted his pet to be the one that killed me and ripped me apart. I thought that this would surely be my end, so I prayed to God with all my heart. My lioness protector stood in front of me, growling and staring at the lion – and the crowd screamed. But the lion wasn't backing down. Next thing I knew, the two magnificent creatures were engaged in a fierce battle – clawing, biting, and roaring for dominance. My lioness fought courageously and intensely, but the lion was very powerful. The fight raged for a long time, each animal exchanging the upper-hand over and over again. The crowd loved it, and cheered wildly. Finally, the two creatures fell to the ground – each was mortally wounded, with blood spattered all over their bodies. And then they both died. My lioness had saved me – but at the cost of her life. I said a silent prayer for her soul.[9]

"Alexander was furious that his prized lion was dead and that I was not. So, he went to the holding pens, opened the gates, and let loose all the wild beasts. The crowd screamed loudly – they knew I no longer had my protector.

"I could sense that this was a bad state of affairs, and that my end could be near. I was sad that I hadn't been able to receive the Holy Spirit, and preach the Gospel to all those who were pure in heart but unenlightened. But I was very happy that I had met Paul, had listened to his sermons, and had accepted the Lord Jesus Christ as my savior. So, I lifted up my arms wide to the sky, tilted my head back, looked straight up to the heavens, and prayed out loud, 'Lord God, heavenly King, O God almighty Father – Lord Jesus Christ, Only Begotten Son – Lord God, Lamb of God, Son of the Father – You take away the sins of the world, have mercy on me,[10] Your unworthy servant.[11] Please forgive this man Alexander, the governor, and all the people who wish me harm. They know not what they do.[12] And please grant blessings to my friend Paul, that he may successfully continue his missionary journeys to bring Your 'Word' to all the world.[13] And please give comfort to my supporter Tryphina, since she has been a blessing to me – and to her daughter Falconilla, that she may reside in heaven by Your side. I ask these things in the name of Jesus, my Lord – Amen.'

"The wild beasts had spotted me and were getting ready to charge. I looked around for help, but all I could see was a large ditch of deep water a few yards away. All I could think in my mind was, *Now is the time for me to be baptized in water – to wash myself in holiness*, so I started to make my way to the ditch.

"But the spectators shouted 'No – don't go there. The ditch is filled with predators.' The governor himself cried out 'The ditch is filled with leopard seals[14] and poisonous snakes – you have no chance.' Then I heard him say to himself, 'What a shame – to think that such beauty is to be devoured by these unclean creatures[15]– what a waste.'

"Notwithstanding their cries or the danger, I was impelled to jump into the water in the ditch; and as I did so, I cried out: 'O my Lord, my God – In the Name of the Father, and of the Son, and of the Holy Spirit, I am baptized on this last day of my life!'[16] The crowd gasped as I splashed into the water, submerged myself, and then rose back to the surface.

"Immediately, I felt an inner peace and calm – I had no fear. And at that very moment, the skies darkened, thunder rumbled across the land, lightning flashed violently in the sky, and rain started pelting down. One of the lightning bolts struck the wooden shack in which I had earlier been imprisoned, and it started up ablaze. The fire quickly spread until flame and smoke covered the whole area around me, and shielded me from view by the spectators. Just as I came up out of the water ditch and moved away, a lightning bolt struck the ditch and all of the seals and snakes were stunned or killed. They were no longer a threat. Everything was in chaos, but I was uninjured – and I felt the Holy Spirit stirring within me![17]

"And then, just as abruptly as it had started, the thunderstorm ended, the rain stopped, the sky cleared, and the smoke dissipated. At that moment, the crowd of spectators saw me emerge unscathed from the smoke and flames, while all the wild animals were either dead or cowering in the corner. God had saved me from the beasts!

"The crowd erupted in noisy acclimation, 'Release the woman! She is under the protection of the gods!' Many of them threw aromatic herbs and spices into the arena, notably spikenard,[18] cassia,[19] amomum,[20] and perfumed ointments. The fragrant aroma wafted thickly over the whole arena, causing all the beasts to become docile and meek, showing no desire to attack me.

"After a short time, Alexander went to the governor and said, 'Let me end this travesty. I have some very terrible bulls – let us bind her feet to them, rile them up, and she will be dragged around the arena in spectacular fashion, until she is dead. The audience will love it!' In a sullen manner, the governor replied, 'Do with her as you wish.'

"So, they then put a cord around my waist, tied my feet together, and lashed me to the necks of two bulls. Many people in the crowd were shouting one thing or another, but

I couldn't make it out. Then, the workers applied red-hot irons to the bulls' genitals, tormenting them, and causing them to howl madly and become ferocious. I started to be dragged on the ground as the bulls became frenzied.

"Now, it was just then that my caretaker Tryphina, who was in the stands, fainted from the whole terrible sight, and appeared as if she was dead to all those around. Many people were disturbed, and I heard many shouts of 'Lady Tryphina is dead!'[21]

"But after only having been dragged a short distance, the rope that had bound me to the bulls shredded and broke. It had been inadvertently burned almost through by the red-hot irons when the bulls were being tormented, and was easily torn asunder once the load was stretched and jostled. I was left standing in the middle of the arena, with only a few nicks and bruises, while the bulls went running around in circles ambivalent to my presence. My waist-cloth was tattered and my appearance was disorderly – but the crowd cheered.

"When the proconsul heard that Tryphina was dead, and saw that I was still alive, he put an immediate stop to the games. He summoned Alexander and told him, 'I have stopped this spectacle because the whole amphitheater is in disarray. We must free this woman! If Caesar hears about the things that have happened here today, then I'm afraid that he will destroy our city, along with us, because his relative Tryphina, a person of royal extract, has died in our arena during our games. This woman has the ear of the gods – maybe she can obtain leniency for us.'

"Alexander then fell down at the feet of the proconsul and cried, 'May the gods have mercy upon me!'

"With that, it was ordered that I be escorted out of the arena and summarily brought before the proconsul. Ten minutes later, still wearing my tattered waist-cloth, we were staring at each other face to face. He looked me up and down, and then said, 'Just who are you, anyway? And what is it about you, that none of the wild beasts can harm you?'

"And I replied to him, 'I am a servant of the Most High God – and as to what it is about me – I am a believer in Jesus Christ, the Son of God, in whom He is well pleased.[22] For that reason, none of the beasts could harm me. He alone is the way to eternal salvation and the foundation of eternal life. He is a refuge to those in distress, a solace to those afflicted, a shelter to those who are lost, and a hope for those in despair. In short, those who believe in him will have happiness and everlasting life. Those who do not believe in him will find suffering and eternal damnation.'

"When the proconsul heard this, he ordered that my garments be brought to me, and said, 'Put on your clothes and go home. Your sentence is commuted. You have served your time.'

"As I put my clothes back on, I said to him, 'He that clothed me when I was naked among the beasts, will in the day of judgment clothe me with salvation. I pray that He clothe you also.'

"The proconsul appeared nervous. He immediately issued a formal edict to the people of the city, that stated:

I RELEASE TO YOU NOW THE WOMAN NAMED THECLA, THE SERVANT OF GOD.

When it was broadcast to the crowd in the amphitheater, most of the people shouted aloud with relief and thanks. The majority were no longer against me, but for me – and that made me feel good. In unison, I could hear them praising God and chanting, 'There is but one God, who is the God of Thecla; the one God who has saved her from the beasts!' Their chanting became so loud and powerful that the whole theatre seemed to shake.

"Apparently, the ruckus caused Tryphina to recover from her swoon. She was not dead, as I had feared. She quickly learned that I was alive and unharmed, and came running with a multitude of others to greet me. When she finally found me, she warmly embraced me with much enthusiasm, saying 'Now I believe there will be a resurrection of the dead – and now I believe that my daughter is alive in heaven. Come home with me Thecla, and all that is mine, I shall give to you.' Hearing this, the others responded with, 'Thanks be to God.'[23]

"And then, taking my hand, we slowly walked back to her house, where we prayed and rejoiced until late in the evening."

NOTES

1. Alexander's hat was a replica of the ornamental headdresses worn by the priestly rank of the imperial legionnaires. The figure of Caesar was prominent on the front. Although just a façade, men of social/political status often wore such attire as a symbol of their seeming importance.

2. Lystra was an important city about 18 miles southwest of Iconium. Today, it is only a ruin. In the 1st century, it was connected with Antioch Pisidia by a direct Roman imperial road, which did not pass through Iconium (there was a separate road from Lystra to Iconium). Paul visited here again on his 2nd and 3rd missionary journeys. A temple of Jupiter (Zeus) stood at the gates, and a heathen college of priests was located there. Being on the imperial road, it was an important Roman military stopping-point. Nearby the present-day village of 'Klistra' are ancient ruins, including a church with a big cross marked on the wall, a winery, and house-like buildings. This thought-to-be site of Lystra is still awaiting serious excavation.

3. Yes, this is the same Timothy that will join Paul on his 2nd missionary journey, and go on to become a lifelong friend, ardent believer, and dedicated evangelist. Reference 2 Timothy 3:10-17 and 4:1-5.

4. The amphitheater was intended to be used for animal fights and gladiatorial combats, but was also used for public executions on occasion.

5. Falconilla was likely in purgatory, and sought intercession by the saints for her purification and elevation into heaven.

6. A parallel case to the prayer of Saint Thecla for the unbaptized and deceased Falconilla, is the prayer by Saint Perpetua for the unbaptized and deceased Dinocrates, her brother.

7. The contrarians were in the minority, and were mostly women.

8. A waist-cloth (also called a loincloth, when pertaining to men) was a common undergarment in the hotter regions of the Roman Empire in the first century. It was a short skirt that wrapped around the hips and reached about halfway down the thighs. It was usually kept in place by tucking, although sometimes a belt was used. At times, it was worn alone.

9. All living things have a soul. The more complex the creature, the more complex (or advanced) the soul. The human being has the most complex soul, but also has a spirit given to it by God at conception. The spirit is the center of God consciousness, unavailable to all lower forms of life.

10. Thecla's prayer is a precursor to the 'Gloria' (an ancient hymn of praise) in the Catholic liturgy, and the 'Gloria in Excelsis' in the Protestant service.

11. "Your unworthy servant" is a term used in the Eucharistic Prayer in the Catholic liturgy, usually self-referring to a bishop, cardinal, or pope.

12. This, of course, is analogous to Jesus' renowned saying while suffering on the cross. Reference Luke 23:34.

13. By referring to the 'Word', Thecla means the Gospel and the Good News of Jesus Christ. She may not have fully understood that Jesus, himself, was the 'Word of God', the Second Person of the Holy Trinity.

14. Leopard seals are the only seals known to regularly hunt and kill warm-blooded prey, including other seals. Although rare, there are a few records of adult leopard seals attacking humans. There has been at least one recorded fatality, when a researcher was snorkeling in Antarctic waters and was killed by a leopard seal.

15. Like the Jews, the pagan Romans considered many creatures to be 'unclean' (although not the same specific ones). It wasn't just about their use as food, but also about their use as pets, or work-things, or using their body parts in products after death. Just touching an 'unclean' creature could sometimes be sacrilegious. Seals and snakes were considered 'unclean'. See Leviticus 11 for a more complete Jewish listing.

16. Thecla baptized herself under the pretext that Paul would have baptized her if she had lived. She felt justified in doing this, even though only a person who had already received the Holy Spirit could be a baptizer, since she believed that she was only moments away from death.

17. Significantly, by becoming baptized, Thecla believed that her covenant with God bound her to live a celibate life.

18. Also called nard or muskroot, spikenard was a costly aromatic ointment, preserved in alabaster boxes, whose chief ingredient was derived from a flowering plant of the valerian family. It has a strong musky, earthy, or woodsy aroma, similar to that of valerian root.

19. Cassia is a relative of cinnamon, both coming from the bark of a tree that is a member of the laurel family. It has a similar, but stronger, aroma and flavor than cinnamon. It was an ingredient in anointing oil, as described in Exodus 30:22–25. Cassia is one of the oldest known spices to mankind, having been used for thousands of years to maintain physical health and promote emotional well-being.

20. Amomum is a plant in the ginger family, similar to cardamom. The seeds are strongly aromatic, with hints of sweet, sour, bitter, salty, and spicy taste. A grain of amomum in a dish being steamed can fill a house with its fragrance.

21. Tryphina's formal title was Queen Antonia Tryphina, but she was known as 'Lady Magnificent'– a relative of the Emperor Claudius, who ordained that a part of the province of Cilicia be given to her first son Polemo II. Whether or not he was ever mentioned to Thecla, is unknown.

22. Note the similarity to the baptism of Jesus. See Matthew 3:17 or Luke 3:22.

23. A lay response in the Catholic liturgy

3 FAITH CONDEMNED AND SUSTAINED IN LYSTRA

"Form a circle of protection — Let no harm come to Paul, for he is a servant of God"

THE PLACE is in the house of Timothy in the city of Lystra, just south of Iconium.

THE SETTING: Thecla has returned from Antioch with friends and has related the story of her persecution, torture, and baptism there to Paul, Barnabas, and Timothy.

AFTER listening to Thecla's story, everyone was amazed, relieved, and thankful, all at once. Her presence among them was the shining light in an otherwise dreary sequence of events in trying to proclaim the Gospel. Timothy asked her how and why she decided to come to Lystra. And so, Thecla concluded the story of her adventure in Antioch:

"For two days, I stayed in the house of Tryphina, teaching the holy Gospel and the ways of the Lord to her and the maidservants. They became true believers and I praised God for that blessing.

"But I yearned to see Paul again and learn more from my respected mentor. So, I inquired through all the channels of travel and commerce available, and at length, was informed that two men fitting your descriptions were here in Lystra. I just knew that it had to be you. So, I gathered together all the believers and friends from the household, and we set out for Lystra as soon as we could. I had already decided that my presence as a woman could be a hindrance, so I sewed my clothes together to look like a man's coat, and cut my hair so as to have the appearance of a man. My female traveling companions did the same. As such, we had no troubles and arrived here quickly and safely."

The whole group rejoiced greatly, and agreed to go out with renewed vigor to preach the Gospel the next day. They decided to start by going into the town square at the height of the shopping time when many people would be present. And so, they all retired and slept peacefully, content in the knowledge that as a group, their teaching efforts would be that much more productive.

HEALING OF THE LAME

BRIGHT and fresh the next day, the group headed out to the town square – Paul, Barnabas, Timothy, Thecla, and her compatriots. Barnabas and Thecla were the main spokespersons, gathering people's attention and having them focus that attention on Paul, who did the actual preaching. Their results were modest. A few people stopped to listen, but most just ignored them and continued on their way. After all, many other odd self-proclaimed magicians, sorcerers, messiahs, and prophets had addressed folks in the town square, since Lystra was a large trading hub, religious center, and military stopover. Paul was just another one of many.

That afternoon, a man came by on crutches and assisted by relatives. He was totally lame, unable to walk by himself. They sat him down in the shade in the square, as was their custom to do, and then they went off about their business.

He was not far from Paul, and could hear him clearly. He listened to the teaching with rapt attention, and was captivated by Paul's message. But he didn't say anything. He just stared at Paul with an expression of longing. He hungered for the taste of a new life – one without pain and suffering – and so he sat spellbound, soaking in the pious words of Paul.

Eventually, their eyes met and Paul looked into the heart and soul of the cripple. He sensed that the man was pure in heart and strong in faith.

"You, over there – what is your name?" he asked in a loud voice.

Startled, the man wasn't sure at first if he was the intended recipient of the enquiry, and pointed to himself in questioning fashion. When Paul acknowledged that yes, he was the one to whom the question was aimed, he said humbly, "My name is Lycius."

Then Paul continued: "Lycius, my friend. I sense that you are an honorable man. Are you happy? Do you believe that the gods protect you and help you?"

Lycius stammered but was finally able to mumble, "I have come to peace with my handicap."[1]

Then Paul replied, "If you believe in the Lord Jesus Christ as your one and only savior and forgiver of sins, with all your heart and all your mind, then you will be saved. Your sins will be forgiven and you will be resurrected on the last day with a new glorified body and live forever in peace and happiness. Lycius, do you believe this?"

After a few seconds of silence, Lycius blurted out, "Yes, I believe. I believe. My Lord, and my God."[2]

"Then rise up on your feet, and walk my friend! Your faith has healed you!"[3]

Within a few seconds, the man's countenance changed, his body swelled with pride, and he stood up – and walked. He was exuberant with joy, and shortly began to jump and dance about. "Look at me. I can walk," he shouted, giddy with glee. "I can walk! I can walk! O my God, I give you thanks – I give you everything!"

Now, all those in the small gathered crowd saw and heard everything that had happened, and they were astonished. Many of them befriended the man and patted him on the back. Many rushed off, scurrying here and there, to tell the whole city about the miracle. Before long, a large enthusiastic crowd had gathered.

Paul and Barnabas were busy talking, answering questions, and exchanging greetings, when suddenly a man in the crowd shouted out, "Hail! The gods have come to us in the form of men! Zeus, we praise you! Hermes, we salute you! Glory to Zeus and Hermes! Glory to the gods!"

Within seconds, the whole square was filled with acclamation and reverence. Everyone was bestowing worship and praise on Paul and Barnabas, while simultaneously asking for favor for their specific needs and hardships.

They called Barnabas 'Zeus', because he brought the power of the gods down to earth. They called Paul 'Hermes', because he brought the message of healing directly to a mortal being.

The crowd became more and more excited and frantic as more and more people tried to gain the indulgence of the gods. Paul and Barnabas were caught up in a frenzy of exaltation and supplication. Even the high priest from the temple that stood outside the town square brought garlands of fruits and flowers,[4] and even fattened oxen, to the square and placed them before Paul and Barnabas. He wished to offer a sacrifice to the gods (and for everyone to see him doing so). It seemed that every person in the city was showering them with adulation.[5]

Of course, Paul and Barnabas were horrified once they realized what was going on. They stepped off the soapbox and rushed into the crowd, crying "Friends, do not do this! We are only mortal human beings, just like you! We just want to bring you the Good News that will convert you to the true God – the One who made heaven and earth, the sea and the sky, and everything that is in them – and the One who would frown on follies such as this!"

Timothy and Thecla tried to help but their voices were drowned out by the raucous noise of the crowd. But Paul continued to shout out:

"In the past, God let the Gentiles go their own way. But He has not hidden Himself completely from you. He has bestowed benefits on you! From the heavens He sends down rain for rich harvests, such that your body and spirit is filled with food and delight. Now He has taken human form and come down to earth to forgive your sins and give you eternal life. All you have to do is believe in Him! I am just a voice in the wilderness that teaches this. I have seen Him! Listen to me!"

But it was to no avail. Hardly anyone heard him. And the crowd continued with adoration and praise, many offering small sacrifices at their feet.

THE STONING

IT was just then that a bunch of people, mostly Jews from Antioch and Iconium, arrived on the scene. They knew about Paul and Barnabas from when they had visited their cities, and they were appalled at this exposition of god-worship by the people of Lystra. They waded into the crowd, waving their arms and shouting:

"Citizens of Lystra – STOP – these men are no gods! We have seen them before in our cities. They are charlatans! This one here," pointing to Paul, "practices black magic and sorcery. He brainwashes our youth by telling them to reject marriage, religious laws, and cultural norms. And he does not respect the gods of Rome!"

The Jews said this, not because they believed in the Roman gods, but because they discerned that the Jesus cult presented a threat to the constancy of the Hebrew religion.[6]

Gradually, they began to win over the crowd, and there was rampant confusion all around. Then they shouted loudly, "These men are no friends of Rome. This one disrespects the Roman people, belittles the Roman laws, and defames the Roman gods! For your own good, send him away! Punish him so he won't return! Stone him!"

With that, most of the crowd changed their attitude and became hostile to Paul and Barnabas. Their reverence turned to wrath, and they became angry and irritated. It grew worse and worse until finally they started to push, shove, and otherwise hustle Paul out of the town square. Barnabas, Timothy, and Thecla were powerless against the multitude.

When they got to a clearing some blocks from the square, they became riled up by the vocal agitators, and one of the citizens clamored, "This man is a heathen! He should die! Stone him!". Whereupon many of them started to pick up rocks and throw them at Paul.

At this point, Thecla could stand no more. She shouted at the top of her lungs, "I call to all friends and believers in the Most High God and our Lord Jesus Christ! We must save this holy man! Form a circle of protection – Let no harm come to Paul, for he is a servant of God!"

Then, Barnabas, Timothy, Thecla, her followers from Iconium, and a few ardent disciples joined hands and formed a human ring around Paul, and prevented most of the rocks from hitting him.[7] Many of them became bruised and battered, but after a while it became apparent to the unruly crowd that they could not injure or kill this man. It was nearing dinner time anyway, and they had successfully made their point, roughed him up, and ushered him out of the center of town – good enough. Eventually, the crowd dispersed.

Slowly, the believers gathered their wits and belongings together, rubbed their wounds, and made their way back to the house of Timothy – just another day that didn't turn out as hoped.

SEPARATE WAYS

THAT evening, they all discussed what they should do next. Continuing on in Lystra was probably not a good idea. Like Antioch and Iconium, they had met stiff opposition from some Jews and from some Gentile officials. Yes, they had reached some people and perhaps made a few converts, but the enduring efficacy of the mission was uncertain.

Barnabas wanted to return to Perga and the nearby seaport from which they had entered Pamphylia from Cyprus.[8] But Paul wanted to continue southeastward to Derbe, which was in the direction, and not too far, from his hometown of Tarsus.[9] But Thecla's friends and followers wanted to return to Antioch – and she was inclined to return to Iconium to see her mother.

"I cannot go with you to Derbe," she sighed. "My friends are anxious to return home to Antioch, and I must go with them. But I promise to meet with you again, to learn more about the Gospel, and to share in the work of bringing people to God."

"Yes, of course," said Paul. "You have done well in the eyes of God. Your faith is strong, my friend – and you must stay the course. If you do this, you will find reward both on earth and in heaven.

"Timothy, you should stay here and help the small

number of believers establish a local church. I may pass through Lystra again in the future, and will need a good friend and fellow believer.[10]

"So, it is up to you, Barnabas. Will you accompany me to Derbe? There are new people to meet,[11] teaching to be done, conversions to be made, and churches to set up. The work is tough, but it is the will and commission of our Lord."

Reluctantly, Barnabas agreed to go to Derbe.

The next morning after breakfast, Paul gave them all a special blessing: "May the grace of our Lord Jesus Christ be with you all."[12] And with that, they all bid their farewells and departed, each going their separate ways.

NOTES

---

1. Lycius had been lame from birth, never having walked in his life.

2. Compare with the exclamation of the Apostle Thomas in John 20:26-29.

3. The story of Paul's healing of the lame man is aptly described in Acts 14:8-18.

4. At the entrance to the main part of town stood a magnificent pagan temple next to a large statue of Zeus. Many priests and supplicants lived in the adjoining buildings.

5. In an effort to convince the people that divine power works through belief in the Word of God, Paul heals the cripple. But the pagan tradition of occasional appearance of gods among mortals leads the people astray in interpreting the miracle. This incident reveals the cultural difficulties with which the early church had to cope – difficulties that have remained for thousands of years, even until today.

6. The term 'Christians' (which was coined in Syrian Antioch – see Acts 11:26) was still new and not yet in widespread use in outlying regions.

7. The stoning of Paul and his rescue by disciples is described in Acts 14:19-20.

8. On the First Missionary Journey, Paul, Barnabas, and John Mark sailed from Paphos on the island of Cyprus (where the proconsular governor Sergius Paulus was converted – see Acts 13:6-7) to Perga in the region of Pamphylia on the southern coast of Anatolia. It was here that John Mark left them and returned to Jerusalem.

9. Paul was known as 'Saul of Tarsus' before his conversion from Christian persecutor to Christian missionary.

10. Paul and Silas reach Lystra on the Second Missionary Journey in 51 AD, where Timothy joins them en-route to Asia Minor, Macedonia, and Greece.

11. The native people in the region were of a distinct racial group known as Lycaonians, who spoke a peculiar dialect. Many of them were lawless opportunists, speculators, and fortune hunters. Paul recognized the need to reach them, but understood the difficulty that would be involved.

12. Compare with Revelation 22:21.

4 FAITH SUPPORTED AND ENCOURAGED IN MYRA

"Go forth into the world and teach the Gospel, in the Name of the Father, and of the Son, and of the Holy Spirit"

THE YEAR is 60 AD.

THE PLACE is in the house of Hermias in the city of Myra,[1] in the province of Lycia on the southern coast of Anatolia.

THE SETTING: Paul has completed his three missionary journeys and is now under Roman house arrest because of charges brought by the Jerusalem temple High Priest, supported by accusations of Jewish leaders from the Asian provinces where he had earlier visited and preached. Under guard, he has been put on a sailing ship headed for Rome because, as a Roman citizen, he has appealed his case to the jurisdiction of the Emperor, rather than being tried locally in Jerusalem where Jewish henchmen were waiting to kill him. He is escorted by the Roman centurion Julius and accompanied by fellow Christian prisoner Aristarchus on the journey.[2] The ship has docked in the port of Myra, where arrangements are being made for transfer to another ship bound for Italy. Until the new ship is readied and arrangements complete, Paul has been given permission to stay locally in the house of a friend, while being guarded by Julius.

IN THE HOUSE OF HERMIAS

PAUL has been given a certain amount of leniency because of his citizenship status. As such, he has been allowed to stay off-ship while arrangements are being made to continue the voyage. The Roman centurion Julius keeps a watch on him 24-7, but he is otherwise free to move about. It's been three days since the ship docked in Myra and they have been staying at the home of Hermias, who became a disciple of Christ before Paul.[3]

"We will probably be ready to sail in three or four days," remarked Julius. "I will be glad when we get to Rome and back to civilization," said he with a wink of an eye.

For his part, Paul presented little problem for Julius. There was no animosity or rancor between them. In fact, Julius respected Paul, and recognized his intelligence and prophetic insight.[4] Fellow believers often came to visit and long hours were spent discussing the Good News, as well as the civil/political situation in Jerusalem.

On the fourth day, there was a knock on the door, but it wasn't one of the visiting believers. It was Thecla, accompanied by two friends!

"Greetings to all, and especially to Paul, my friend, teacher, and guide to the Gospel of our Lord, Jesus Christ. I am so happy to have found you! To almighty God, Creator of heaven and earth, I give you praise for allowing me to see Paul again."

"Thecla, I am very happy to see that you are well and in good spirits!" exclaimed a surprised but somber Paul. "How did you learn I was here? Where are you living now? What happened after you left Lystra?"

"I am in Seleucia in Cilicia now.[5] These are my friends from there and fellow believers, Episteme and Therasia. They are disciples of Christ. We have established a community and a church on the hillside on the outskirts of town,[6] where we are mostly self-sufficient and united in faith.

"We go into the city every now and then for food, supplies, and news. As I have been on the lookout for any word about you ever since we departed, always hoping that one day I could see you again, I was intrigued when one quiet afternoon near the pagan religious center, I heard some men talking about a Roman citizen who was a follower and promoter of the Nazorean Jesus cult – who started a riot in the temple in Jerusalem and was arrested by the authorities – who had appealed to the Emperor for justice – and had been sent to Rome accordingly. When they said they thought his name was Paul, I was very interested and curious!

"So, I went to the port transportation, commerce, and shipping office and inquired about any ships that would be sailing from Judea to Rome carrying a prisoner named Paul. And by the grace of God, sure enough, they found it and told me that it had just docked in Myra for a week for repairs.

"My heart began to race. I knew that it had to be you, although I doubted the reasons for the incarceration. And I knew that this might be the last chance I might ever have of seeing you again. So, I quickly gathered together whatever belongings I could, and made my way here as fast as possible. Thankfully, my kind and gracious friends Episteme and Therasia insisted on accompanying me.

"And so here we are. And look at you – under guard and unable to openly preach the Gospel! Have they hurt you? Are you healthy?"

"I am fine," said Paul. "Just the usual aches, pains, bumps, and bruises."

"But please," insisted Thecla, "you must tell us everything you've done in the last 10 years – the places you've been, the sights you've seen, and the things you have done – the whole story."

And so, for the next two hours, Paul related the extraordinary story of his three missionary journeys followed by his troubles with the Jewish and Roman authorities in Jerusalem and Caesarea.[7]

"So that's about it. It's been clear to me for some time that Jesus called me primarily to bring the Good News to the Gentiles, and I've pursued that to the best of my abilities. But my mission isn't over. I feel that I must go to Rome, and then on to Spain, to better reach the Gentile world. So, Rome is my next stop. Of course, I'd rather be traveling as a free man rather than as a prisoner – but I'm traveling – and will spread the Gospel with all of my strength. That was the commission of our Lord,[8] and that is my life's work."

Hermias, Aristarchus, Julius, and Thecla listened intently and marveled at the amazing story.

Finally, Julius uttered, "You are a remarkable man, Paul."

Dodging the flattery, Paul replied, "But tell us, Thecla, everything that has happened to you since I saw you last – when we all left Lystra and went our separate ways. I'm so glad you are strong and healthy, but I'm dying to know your story. You are young, gifted, and have God's protection. Tell us how you came to Seleucia."

"My faith and my works pale in comparison to my esteemed teacher. I am not worthy to share the storytelling stage with him," she replied.

"But please, indulge us. We really want to hear. After everything you've already been through, we just have to know the rest of the story."[9]

And so, Thecla began to tell her story:

THE LAST JOURNEY

"**AFTER** leaving Lystra, our return to Antioch was uneventful. Tryphina was especially glad to see me, and we were all given a royal welcome home. But after a few weeks, I needed to return to Iconium – I had to see my mother again. And so, I hired passage with a transport service, and rode in a horse-drawn carriage from Antioch to Iconium. Tryphina had given me a large sum of money, clothes, food, and other necessities for the trip."

"When I arrived in the city, I immediately went to my house in the town square and greeted my mother. She looked well and I was happy to see her, but she pretended that she didn't know me.

'Mother, it is I, your daughter Thecla, you know it is me! My hair and my clothes cannot disguise me from you. I have returned from my travels. I have learned the ways of God and have suffered much persecution. My faith has been tested but I did not falter. Now I am home and we can be together again.'

'I have no daughter,' she replied. 'I do not know who you are. Get out of my house!'

'But mother, you know it is me – she who has been your daughter for 18 years – I am home! And I'm very glad to see you. I love you regardless of your beliefs and past actions. Can't you receive me despite my actions and beliefs?'

"And again she replied, 'I have no daughter. I do not know who you are. Get out of my house! I believe only in the ways of the Roman gods – that is how it has always been and how it will always be.'

'But mother, is it possible for you to be brought to a belief that there is but one Lord God Almighty? And that His only begotten Son came down to earth for the forgiveness of our sins, and to enable us to have everlasting life in heaven? I believe it – Amen. Can you also believe? If you desire riches and happiness, God can give them to you. And if you want your daughter again, here I am.'

"But she just stared out into nothingness, and said 'My daughter is dead. I do not know who you are. Get out of my house! I believe only in the ways of the Roman gods – that is how it has always been and how it will always be.' "

"Weeping and saddened beyond words, I left my house and wandered across the square to the house of Onesiphorus. But there was no one home, and it appeared to be empty. The door was open and so I went in – sure enough, the house was vacant – no goods, no supplies, no furniture. I went into the large room facing the square and threw myself down on the floor – the very spot where Paul had sat and preached. Choked with tears and emotion, I cried and prayed for a long time, finishing with the simple words:

'O my God – the God of this house – the house in which the Light did first shine upon me – O Lord Jesus, Son of the living God, Who was my helper before the governor, my helper in the fire, and my helper among the beasts – You alone are my God forever and ever. Glory is Your name! Have mercy on me, Your humble servant. Amen.'

"When I enquired with a neighbor, he said that the family of Onesiphorus had moved to Ephesus.[10] They had been ostracized by the community and he was fearful of the children's well-being.

"I then asked that same neighbor, if he knew anything about Thamyris. And he told me that Thamyris was dead. His public humiliation had been too much to bear and he had sought refuge in the low-end drink-houses. Apparently, one night he got embroiled in a bitter dispute, a fight ensued, and he was killed.

"So, I prayed to God with all my heart, and sincerely asked that he be forgiven for what he had done to me. At that moment I also asked God to forgive my mother, and prayed that she be kept safe and well so that one day she would see the Light and believe in God. I bowed my head, marked my body in a cruciform motion with the sign of the cross,[11] and wandered off out of the town, sad and dejected."

"Without consciously realizing it, I wandered out near the cave on the road to Daphne – the same cave where I had earlier met up with Paul and Barnabas. When I saw it, I sensed the kindness and approachability that emanated from it, and so I quickly went straight to it and proceeded in. Once inside the cave, I was completely overcome with my emotions, and I dropped to the ground sobbing and wailing. So many emotions – so many remembrances! And I wept and prayed the whole night until early morning, catching only a few winks during the night.

"The next morning was dark and heavily overcast. It seemed that at any moment, the sky would burst open with rain, wind, thunder, and lightning. But then, amidst the darkened canopy, a bright cloud appeared directly over the entrance to the cave. It was white as snow and had a shimmering golden haze all around it. A beam of sparkling silver light radiated from it, rising straight up into heaven. It was the most magnificent sight I had ever seen."

"It began to move, and I was drawn to follow it. At first, I thought it might just lead me a short way – maybe to a clearing or field – I wasn't sure what its significance was. But it kept moving and moving, and I kept following and following. I passed some hamlets and villages and noticed that the people there did not appear to see the cloud. I couldn't understand why – it was so brilliant and splendid –

they seemed to think that I was disturbed or deranged. Here I was, walking along with my head tilted back and eyes raised, fixated upon the resplendent cloud – a cloud that no one else could see. Although I didn't think it then, I must have looked very strange. So they mostly shunned me – left me alone, since I wasn't interfering with their daily activities – and I just kept watching and walking, following the majestic cloud with its silver tether to heaven.

"I followed the cloud for five days, walking about 10 hours a day.[12] I don't know why I kept going – I just felt I had to. Every night when I fell asleep, I thought the cloud would be gone the next morning. But it was always right there where I stopped – and started up again the next day.

"The cloud led me to the outskirts of the seaport town of Seleucia in Cilicia,[13] at which point it vanished in an evanescent wisp of smokey haze rising straight up. Of course, by then I knew that the cloud was a sign from God. This is where He wanted me to be – His will be done. And so, I was content.

"I walked into the town and took a room in the inn."

IN SELEUCIA

"THE next day I went to the town square and started to talk to people about God, life, salvation, and resurrection – all the things I had learned from Paul. I tried to speak as Paul did, with the same conviction and sense of purpose.

"But I was not received – all I got were hoots and catcalls. Dressing as a man couldn't hide my womanhood, and I was shouted off with curses and threats. I was so dejected. I wanted so badly to tell them the Good News, but they just wouldn't listen. A female talking about the one true God was simply not acceptable behavior. I had to slink away quickly or I would have been beaten and maybe killed – I'm sure of it.

"Crestfallen, I wandered out to the edge of town. And there – wonder of wonders – I saw the same majestic white cloud with the silver beam up to heaven. It began to move west and I followed it.

"After less than a mile, it stopped over a small mountain range [14]– and then it disappeared again. *This must be where God wants me to be*, I thought. The slope was gradual, and on the eastward side there appeared to be many small caves. So, I walked up to the mountainside caves and saw that they were empty – not infested with bats, animals, or rodents. After exploring a few of the caves, I selected one as the place where I would sleep and live – at least temporarily. I would watch for the cloud again, and follow it if it appeared.

"But the next day, the cloud did not appear – Nor the next week or the next month. Apparently, this is where I was meant to be. So, for the next few months I worked on transforming the cave into a home."

"Now, it turns out, that some children who had heard me in the square, and saw that I was harassed and hurried out of town, followed me and noticed that I went into the caves outside of town. Evidently, they told their parents that a strange woman in the town square had to retreat to the caves to escape maltreatment. Upon hearing this, some of the more gentlewomen of the town were concerned, so they came out to my cave to see who I was, and if I had been harmed at all. They were much more receptive to hearing my story and learning about the one true God and our Lord Jesus Christ, than were the men in the town square.

"It quickly became obvious that we had common interests and desires, and we found it easy to talk to each other – we hit it off, so to speak. We became friends and they became regular visitors. They would bring me food and accessories, and I would teach them about the ways and miracles of God.

Eventually, many of them abandoned their life in the city, and joined with me in the surrounding caves to lead an ascetic life. Thanks be to God, they converted to Christ, I baptized them, and we now live in a righteous God-loving community. Episteme and Therasia have been with me since that time."

"One day, a woman who I had not seen before, came to my cave and brought with her a sick child. He had a fever and was not eating or drinking. The doctors in the town were unable to do anything, and she had heard from others about the miracles of God that I had preached. So, I talked to her and she listened patiently – she was sincere and ready to believe.

"I said to her, 'Do you believe in the one true God, and in His only begotten Son, our Lord Jesus Christ, who forgives our sins and delivers us from all evil?'

'I do,' she said.

"Then I touched the child on his forehead with my holy water,[15] and said 'Rise up my child! Away with this fever and sickness! May the devil be cast out of you! In the Name of the Father, and of the Son, and of the Holy Spirit, I command the release of this child! Be well and be thankful to God!'

"With that, the fever left the child and he was made whole again. The mother was so thankful, that she showered me with gifts and ran off to tell her friends and relatives the good news. She has since become an ardent supporter of our community.

"I felt so good after that – fulfilled and happy. But to tell you the truth, I was very nervous at first. I had some self-doubts and my faith wavered. But then I looked at the innocence of the child and the goodness of the woman. I sensed the honesty, decency, and morality in her heart, and in an instant I was filled with the Holy Spirit, and felt totally in touch with God. I just straightaway did what my heart said to do. It was an amazing experience!

"And from this, a good report was spread throughout the town of the strange woman in the cave."

THE COMMISSION

"**AND** so, that is my story – everything that has happened to me since when we separated in Lystra. I am not the teacher or the hero that Paul is – I have just tried to do my best and remain faithful to God, and to all the teachings that I have learned."

Everyone in the room was both awed and humbled by the acts of Paul and Thecla. For a long while, they all sat in meditation, prayed, and engaged in quiet conversation.

After a time, Julius was called away. When he returned, he said that they would probably have to return to the ship on the morrow because it was nearing readiness.

"I'm so glad to have seen you again," said Thecla. "maybe I can visit with you again in Rome. After all, all roads lead to Rome."[16]

"Maybe so," said Paul. "But for now, your mission is in Pamphylia, Lycaonia, and Galatia.[17] Go there and preach the Word of God. And later – only God knows – just listen for His calling!"

After a moment of silence, Paul continued: "Thecla, my friend, you have my blessing. Go forth into the world and teach the Gospel, in the Name of the Father, and of the Son, and of the Holy Spirit."

Then, the room fell quiet and everyone slowly drifted off to sleep while saying their private prayers.

The next morning, Paul, Julius, and Aristarchus left to return to the ship and Thecla, Episteme, and Therasia left to return to Seleucia.

NOTES

1. Myra was an ancient Greek, then Roman, then Byzantine, then Ottoman town in the province of Lycia, which became the small Turkish town of Kale, renamed Demre in 2005 (although it's still signposted as Kale), in the present-day Antalya Province of Turkey. By the late 4th century AD, Myra had grown to be the capital of Lycia. Being the most important city of Lycia, Myra had its own bishop – and this was the renowned Saint Nicholas. Nicholas was born the son of a wealthy merchant. Upon the death of his father, Nicholas spent his inheritance helping the poor and needy. One of his deeds was to give anonymous gifts to dowry-less village girls. To do that, he dropped bags of coins down the chimneys of their houses. This gift from heaven allowed them to marry. After his death, Saint Nicholas became the patron saint of Greece, Russia, children, unmarried girls, etc. Many towns and cities were named after him, such as Sint-Niklaas in Belgium. In Dutch, his name became corrupted to Sinterklaas. But it was the Americans who finally merged the good saint with the pagan Father Christmas, to create the well-known Santa Claus.

A majority of Christian Greeks lived in Demre until the 1920s. In 1923, the city's Greek inhabitants were required to leave by the Population Exchange agreement between Greece and Turkey, at which time its celebrated church was finally abandoned. The abandoned Greek houses in the region are a striking reminder of this exodus. Even a Greek ghost town can still be seen there. A small population of Turkish farmers moved into the region when the Greek people migrated out. The region is popular with tourists today, particularly Christian pilgrims who visit the tomb of Saint Nicholas.

2. Aristarchus was with Paul in Ephesus at the 'riot of the silversmiths' on the second missionary journey (Acts 19:29), and eventually became a co-prisoner with him in Rome (Colossians 4:10).

3. Hermias was one of the 70 original disciples in Jerusalem, but left shortly after the resurrection of Jesus due to persecution by the Jewish authorities. At this time, many of the disciples fled out of Judea and started fledgling churches abroad.

4. Julius stood up for Paul on a number of occasions, most noteworthy being during the great storm at sea, when the ship was being torn apart, and the soldiers onboard wanted to kill the prisoners so they couldn't escape by swimming away. Julius opposed that plan and instead commanded an orderly evacuation of all hands (Acts 27:39-44).

5. Seleucia Cilicia is not to be confused with Seleucia Pieria in Syria, which was the port for the major city of Antioch in Syria, from which Paul departed on his first missionary journey. Seleucia Cilicia was a city in the Roman province of Cilicia, in southcentral Anatolia (modern-day Turkey), and was also known as 'Seleucia on the Calycadnus' (a nearby river and valley). It was near the Mediterranean coast and achieved considerable commercial prosperity as a port,

rivaling that of Tarsus. In the 2nd century it became a religious center, with a renowned Temple of Jupiter, and the site of a noted school of philosophy and literature. After the Roman recognition and tolerance of Christianity, bishops held a 'Council of Seleucia' in 325, 359, and 410 AD. By 732 AD, nearly all of the province of Cilicia (then called Isauria) was incorporated into the Patriarchate of Constantinople. The city fell in 1375 to the Egyptian Mamelukes and in 1515 to the Ottoman Turks. Noteworthy is the fact that during the Third Crusade, the celebrated Frederick Barbarossa was drowned in the river there.

6. Actually, in a complex of ancient caves in the nearby mountains – Thecla was abridging the explanation. Archeological evidence of residency in these caves by early Christians remains to this day.

7. The entire story, inspired by God and probably written by Luke, is covered in Acts 13:1 through 27:5.

8. Matthew 28:16-20.

9. Of course, the story that Thecla relates, is not the end of her story. There is more yet to come.

10. Onesiphorus had his new home at Ephesus, and had met up with Paul there on his 2nd and 3rd missionary journeys. He was very kind to Paul, even traveling to Rome to visit him when he was in prison there. Paul mentions him in terms of grateful love – as having a noble courage and generosity on his behalf, amid his trials as a prisoner in Rome, when others from whom he expected better things had deserted him. It was to Paul that the church at Ephesus owed its origin, and it was to Paul that the Christians there were indebted for all that they knew about Christ. Though Onesiphorus had come to Rome, his household had remained in Ephesus; and a last salutation is sent to them by Paul. He could not write again, as he was now very near to execution. But as he writes, he entertains the kindest feelings toward Onesiphorus and his household, and he prays that the Lord will give mercy to them all (Refer to 2 Timothy 1:16-18). According to tradition, Onesiphorus was later martyred by being tied to horses and then torn apart.

11. It is unknown if this was taught to Thecla by Paul, or whether she discovered it on her own.

12. Thecla walked 155 miles in 51 hours altogether.

13. Today, Seleucia Cilicia is called Silifke, a city in the Mersin province of Turkey. It is located at 36.38 deg. latitude : 33.93 deg. longitude, at an elevation of ~56 feet above sea level. Silifke has a population of about 75,000. It's a short distance north of the seaport of Taşucu. It was founded by Seleucus I Nicator (one of Alexander the Great's generals) in the 3rd century BC. In the 5th century AD, the local Byzantine governor had two legions of troops stationed here. West of the town is the Christian cemetery, which contains many tombs of imperial soldiers.

14. Once called Mount Calamon (or Mount Rodeon) and today called Gedik Dagi – a hilly area at the base of the Taurus Mountains. The caves are about 3 miles from the Silifke bus station, off the road from Silifke to Taşucu.

15. Thecla kept some water, she called 'holy water', that she used in her prayers to God, and that she believed had been blessed by the Holy Spirit.

16. Thecla may have been the origin of this medieval sentiment, originally a reference to Roman roads in general and the *Milliarium Aureum* (Golden Milestone) in particular. Earliest literary records place the derivation from a phrase coined by French poet Alain de Lille in 1175, who said "a thousand roads lead a man forever toward Rome" (*Liber Parabolarum*, 1175). Metaphorically, it can mean 'different paths can take one to the same goal'.

17. The regions wherein Thecla had travelled and ministered.

5 FAITH ESTABLISHED AND ASSAULTED IN SELEUCIA

*"Fear not, Thecla, my faithful servant, for I am with you.
Look and see the place which is opened for you"*

THE YEAR is 65 AD.

THE PLACE is in the cave-home of Thecla in the hills outside the city of Seleucia, in the province of Cilicia on the southern coast of Anatolia.

THE SETTING: Thecla has returned to Seleucia and settled in her new 'home'. Over the next few years, the 'young lady in the cave' has become renown for her spiritual wisdom and healing powers. Many people from the city have come to her to be instructed in the oracles of God and many have become illuminated by the Word of the Lord Jesus Christ.[1] And many people have come to her for healing of physical maladies. Following the leadership and example of Thecla, a monastic community of men and women has sprung up in the complex of caves outside the city. The community maintains good relations with the residents of the city and surrounding countryside.

Missing her learning and fellowship interactions with Paul, Thecla has decided to write him a letter. Although she doesn't know his exact situation or precise physical whereabouts, she is determined to write the letter regardless, and send it to the only address that she has, even knowing that he may never get to read it.[2] She peruses it one last time before dropping it in the post:

> To Paul,
> My esteemed teacher, good friend, and fellow missionary in Christ: From your humble servant and faithful student: Thecla
>
> Greetings to you and your good companions Barnabas and Aristarchus, wherever they may be.
>
> I hope you are in good health, good spirits, and preaching the Good News of our Lord and Savior Jesus, the Christ of God.
>
> When we last parted, you were headed to Rome as a prisoner on a ship, and I was going back to Seleucia. I hope you made it to Rome safely. I don't know if you are there now, or have moved on to Spain, or to somewhere else. But this is the only address that I could find, so I pray that someday it reaches you.
>
> Things are good here in Seleucia. We've established a thriving community of faith in the caves outside the city. Many good people have joined with me to give worship and praise to the one true God and our Lord Jesus Christ. We maintain good relations with the residents of the city. They help us with food and supplies and we provide them with spiritual and physical healing whenever we can. More believers and converts to the faith are coming almost every day. The work here is very fulfilling. I yearn to travel and preach, but I believe that God wants me to be here. There is still so much to do, and I will always do my best.
>
> I wish you all the best fortune in your appeal to the Emperor, and in the important endeavor of teaching the Gospel to all people. I sincerely wish that I could join you there and help in proliferating the Good News of Jesus Christ to the Roman people. With God on my side, I hope that one day I will be able to make that wish a reality.
>
> In the name of Jesus the Christ, our Lord and Savior
>
> All the best regards
> Thecla

THE TEMPTATIONS

ONE morning after prayers, Thecla is talking to her five most trusted compatriots about good and evil:

"My dear friends and fellow believers in Christ – Episteme, Athanasia, Cecilia, Basilissa, and Therasia – I have told you before how our loving God deals with good and evil, and why we are so affected by it. I have also told you about all the evil things that happened to me in Antioch and Iconium – the whole story of my trials and punishments – and the finding of relief, happiness, and personal fulfillment in the giving of my life to the one true God. So, I know you have a good understanding. And I know that you know that you must always put your faith in our Lord and God.

"But let me now tell you about something closer to home – that happened right here in our little settlement – something about good and evil – and about how I was sorely tempted three times by the devil. You need to know this because you also will be tempted by the devil, the great Satan – everyone will be – and you must be prepared to stand up to him and turn him away. You see, his goal is to take the souls of all living people and drag them down to hell, where his dominions reside. If you fall to his temptation, you will never be able to experience true everlasting joy and happiness with God in heaven. You have the choice – you can go either way – up or down. But beware! The decisions will not be easy. Satan will use every trick in the book to get your soul – tricks that tug at the core of your personal being."

So, Thecla began to relate to them the story of her three recent encounters with the devil:

First Temptation by Satan

"Shortly after arriving here in Seleucia, the evil Satan appeared to me in the middle of the night in an apparition.

Of course, I didn't know who it was at first. I was lying down when he came with a host of his followers. A flashing fire was in his hands and it bathed everything in a great light. He placed himself near the mouth of my cave and shed so much light into the cave that it gleamed and shined all over me. Then, the multitude began to sing praises.

"I believe that Satan did this, in order to make me think that it was a heavenly light – that his hosts were angels from heaven, and that God had sent them to watch over the cave, and to give me light in the darkness. I think his plan was that when I came out of the cave, I would bow down to him thinking that he was God, and then he would overcome me.

"When I first saw the light, fancying that it was really from God, it strengthened my heart. Trembling, I thought to myself, *O how glorious – the great captivating light, those many songs of praise, and the angelic host standing outside the cave. But I don't know what they are saying, or from where they come, or what the meaning of this light is, or what those praises mean. Why are they here? Why don't they just come into the cave and tell me their purpose?*

"Then I stood up and prayed to God with a fervent heart, saying, 'O God, is there another creator in addition to You, one who has created angels and filled them with light, and who has sent them to keep me in the light? For I see these figures standing at the mouth of the cave, and I don't know who they are. Yet, they are in a great light and sing loud praises. If they are from some other creator, then please tell me. If they are sent by You, then inform me of the reason for which You have sent them.'

"When the wily evil one saw me, he gathered together his followers, partially coalescing them together, and then they all magically re-appeared over me in a majestic cloud of vapor and mist. When I beheld this imposing vision, I thought they were surely angels of the Almighty God who had come to comfort me, or perhaps even bring me back again to Paul. So, I spread out my hands to God, asking Him to help me understand the vision.

"Then Satan, the hater of all good, said to me, 'Greetings Thecla – I am an angel of the great Almighty God – behold the majestic heavenly hosts that surround me. God has sent us to take you to beyond the Great Sea – to the Holy Land and the glistening shores of the Sea of Galilee – and to bathe you in it, thereby baptizing you in the holiest of water, enabling you to be closer to God, and granting you miraculous healing powers.'

"This sounded very appealing but I didn't say anything in return. I was waiting for an answer to my prayer, but none was forthcoming. I think that was because God was once again testing my resolve – waiting to see if I would be overcome, as my mother was, Thamyris was, Alexander was, and the unbelievers in Iconium and Lystra were.

"Then Satan called to me saying, 'Follow us now, and we will take you to the Holy Land and the Sea of Galilee.'

"And so, I followed them at some little distance. But when we came to the high mountain to the north of the city, the Satan drew near to me, and urged me to go up to the very top of the mountain. I think he wanted to kill me by throwing me off the summit – to wipe me from the face of the earth, so that I would not be able to continue my ministry and preach the Gospel to all around me. But I didn't realize that then. So, naively, I climbed to the top.

"At the summit, he said to me, 'Look around and see the beauty – see the magnificent Holy Land in the distance. It's not too far – we can take you there in no time. Do not be afraid my child – remain calm and put your trust in me. Just take a leap into the air and we will catch you and carry you to the Holy Land. It's so easy. But we cannot pick you up from the ground. You must first take the leap. Then we will seize you and carry you straight to the Sea of Galilee. And there you will be refreshed with the glory of God. There's nothing to it. Just take the leap.'

"I was just about to leap, but then I hesitated. Conflicting and confusing thoughts were stirring around in my mind. But Satan continued to reassure me and egg me on. I'm not sure, but I may have weakened a bit and thought how wonderful it would be in the Holy Land. No sooner had these thoughts raced through my mind, when the real miracle occurred!

"In a grand majestic apparition, the Archangel Michael appeared to me in the air above the precipice, and said, 'Fear not, child of God. This is Satan and his evil hosts who are tempting you. He wishes to deceive you as he deceived your tormenters in Antioch and Iconium. Then, he was hidden in the bodies and souls of your persecutors. But now he has come to you in the guise of an angel of light, in order to trick you into worshipping him. He hopes to enthrall you, in the very presence of God. If you jump, then once you do, he will say to you, "If you worship me forever, I will carry you safely back down to earth. But if you refuse, I will drop you and your body will smash into a million pieces on the rocks below." It is all just an evil trick by the evil one.'

"So, in a loud voice I shouted, 'Get behind me Satan. Away with you!.'[3] Seeing that I was meek and without guile, but able to resist the final temptation, the mighty archangel berated Satan in a loud voice, and drove him away along with his followers. I remained standing on the top of the mountain, feeling sheepish and ashamed. Weeping, I then begged God for forgiveness, as I slowly made my way back to my cave-home."

Second Temptation by Satan

"The second visit of Satan occurred about two weeks later, just long enough such that the first visit was not fresh in my memory.

"One morning, as I was returning home from my daily prayer-walk and nature meditation, I perked up to the sense of smoke and the smell of burning grass. To my horror, there was a large fire right in front of the cave entrance. I thought to myself, *Is this merely very bad luck that such an inferno could start just outside my cave, or was it a menacing sign from unbelievers or hoodlums that wanted me dead or gone?*

"But the fire was not from mortals – nor was it an accident. It was from Satan, the devil himself. He had gathered dead trees and dry grasses, brought them to the cave entrance, and set fire to them; with the intent of consuming the cave and everything within it. He wanted to cut me off from my trust in God, so that I would deny Him. But the fire never entered the cave. I think that God sent an invisible angel to prevent that from happening. But the angel could not put out the fire. It burned all day, and I couldn't get into the cave. Unseen, the Satan kept on bringing big pieces of wood and throwing them into the fire, until the flames rose up high and covered the whole cave. He thought that it would consume the cave and everything in it. But the angel of God was guarding it.

"Finally, an Archangel of God came and chased the Satan away, saying 'Leave now! Away with you! Once before you did deceive the servant Thecla, and now you try to destroy her. Were it not for the mercy of God, you and your hosts would have already been wiped off the face of the earth. But know this: – your time will yet come when you will be cast into the Fire of Hell for all eternity.'

"Then Satan fled from before the Archangel. But the fire continued to burn all around the cave. After a few hours the fire had somewhat cooled down, and I tried to get in the cave, but still could not do so because of the intense heat. I was becoming frightened, although I shouldn't have. I had been tortured with fire before. But it seems to have a strange terrifying power all of its own.

"The Archangel of God then said to me, 'Look at this fire! Are the flames and heat any different from the fire at the stake in Iconium? Trust in God and the fire will not harm you. Look how Satan has tried to make you fearful – to make you forget about God. He will mislead you at every step – he is your enemy! It is he who made this fire that was meant to burn you. And why has he done this? Not because he wants to teach you a lesson. What he wants is to make you come out of the light and into the darkness – to go from an exalted state to degradation, from joy to sorrow, and from glory to abasement.

'See this fire kindled by Satan around your cave? You need to know that it will encompass you if you listen to his bidding. He will plague you with fire; and if you follow him, you will go down into hell after you are dead, and remain in torment there forever. Fire will burn all around you and there will be no deliverance from it. Just as you cannot now go into the cave because of the fire, you will not be able to enter the Kingdom of Heaven until you are fully prepared to accept the Lord Jesus Christ as your personal savior, without any misgiving or hesitation.

'You must understand that the devil has put smoke and fire between you and the gift of salvation. There is no way for you to partake of that gift until the Lord Jesus Christ has parted the fire to make a way for you.'

"Then the Archangel of God called out commands to the fire that burned around the cave, and it parted itself asunder, enabling me to pass through it and enter the cave.

"As I was walking into the cave, as a last gasp attempt to offend me, Satan blew into the fire like a whirlwind, and the flames scorched my garment and singed my body. Surprised, but not frightened by this, I realized that it was a reminder that Satan would never give up, and would be ever tempting me, and all the believers.

"The Archangel then put out the burning fire, dousing it with rainwater from a passing storm. But the wounds remained on my body as a reminder.

Third Temptation by Satan

"The worst temptation – at least, I think it was the most heinous – happened just a few days later.

"Satan, the evil one and hater of all good, took the form of a man that looked very much like Paul, my esteemed friend and teacher, only a little older. He passed before me while I was kneeling under a tree gathering herbs, and greeted me with fair words in a voice that sounded like Paul's, but were actually full of deviousness. When I saw his familiar face, and heard his familiar voice, I arose and welcomed him thinking, *Who is this man who looks and sounds so much like Paul? Is he as kind, humble, and enlightened as Paul? Could this actually be Paul, only older and grayer? Should I react like it is him – with a hug maybe? Or should I just act like he is another stranger? What should I do?* I was cheerful because he reminded me of the graciousness of Paul. I wanted it to be him. But what if it wasn't? *Or maybe, another one just like Paul has come to teach me in the ways of God*, I wondered. I did not suspect that he was a Satan in disguise.

"The familiar stranger then said to me in a friendly tone, 'Rejoice Thecla, and be glad. God has sent me here to tell you something that you should do. Don't be afraid. It is a minor thing, yet it is the word of God that He commanded me to tell you. Will you hear it from me and do it? But if you wish not to hear it, I will go away, and He will know that you would not receive His word.'

"When I heard this, I was unsure, but felt that it was wiser to hear the words than not to. And so, I said to him, 'Speak the Word of God, that I may receive it.'

"Then, the gentleman whispered softly to me, 'It has now been some time since you left the house of your mother and turned away from your husband-to-be, but you are still innocent in the ways of passion and love. Now at this time, God has decreed that it is right for you to take a husband from one of the men in the city. Come together with him in love and passion, and in this way you will bear him children. This will comfort you, and drive you away from loneliness, sorrow, and temptation. Now this is not a difficult thing to do, nor is there any offense in it.'

"But when I heard these words from the man, I was greatly troubled. Something didn't seem right, but I couldn't pinpoint it. *I had made a vow of chastity. But was that only meant to be temporary? Would I be sinning against God if I followed the advice?* I thought. *Or is this truly what He wants? If it is not, will He destroy me? If I follow this advice, will I be punished? Will He cast me into the abyss, and plague me there a long time? But maybe it really is what God wants me to do. Certainly, I've thought about it in the past, but I've always been so busy – maybe I just never made the time – never fully considered the option. O my God, how do I know if this man's words are true? How can I know what to do? I cannot be sure! I cannot decide!*

"The man saw that I was hesitant and said, 'It really is for the best – for you now and in the long run. You should swear to me and to God that you will obey His will.'

"It was at that point that the Holy Spirit stirred inside me and made me pull back. Something said, *Be careful – don't do anything hasty – put your trust in the Lord.* It was a great temptation but finally, after much soul-searching, I cut the cord and blurted out, 'No! I will not be tempted! Get behind me, whoever you are!'

"With that, the man turned away, mumbled something unintelligible, and disappeared.

"When I was back in the cave, I spread my hands out to God, beseeching and entreating Him with tears, to forgive me for doubting my vow and His Word. The temptation was powerful, and I almost succumbed. I remained standing and praying for a very long time until I dropped down upon the earth from hunger and thirst.

"In due time, an angel of God appeared to me when I was praying, and said: 'Always beware of Satan. He will use every trick possible to get your soul. And he is relentless. So, you must always be vigilant!' Then the angel disappeared and that was the end of that.

THE REWARDS

THE YEAR is 78 AD.

UNDER the leadership and tutelage of Thecla, over the course of years, life goes on in the monastic community. Prayers are said, chores are done, and careful interactions with the city dwellers are fruitful. Almost daily, someone from the city comes to the cave dwellers for guidance, support, counseling, or healing. And usually, they return feeling better.

In due time, it happens that a prominent woman of the city, named Arete, has become enamored with Thecla and her passion for her religion.[4] She has witnessed the kindness, counseling, and healings first hand, and she is in admiration of the self-sufficiency and successful organization of the community. The fact that a group of mostly women can be committed to their lifestyle and worldview is a novel and inspiring thing to her. Although considered a good Roman citizen and certainly not converted to Christianity, she is in a position to further elevate the standing of the community in the eyes of the average city-dweller.[5] To that end, she has organized an 'awards ceremony' of sorts, in the community's walled outdoor auditorium in a flat area on the hillside by the caves, to reward the pillars of the monastic community.[6] In attendance are the community members and a few respectable, but open-minded, men and women from the city.

Ten young women are introduced, and their lifetime goals and objectives are explained. At the conclusion of the presentation, Thecla leads the singing of a hymn, to which the rest, standing round as a chorus, respond: "I keep myself pure for my holy Bridegroom, and holding a lighted torch, I go to meet my Lord and my God."

In introducing Thecla, Arete designates her a disciple of Paul, a 'world traveler and prominent philosopher'. In her address, she speaks of those who 'ascribe little importance to wealth, social status, political importance, racial identity, or marriage – and who are ready to yield their bodies to wild beasts and to the fire, because of their yearning and enthusiasm for the things that are of supernatural nature'.[7] She then gives a brief recap of Thecla's persecution and perseverance in Antioch and Iconium.

After finishing the talk, Arete cannot suppress her admiration – she has heard of many acts of Thecla in addition to what she has just described – and so she adds: "And I know that her wisdom and caring has led to many other noble actions. But the things that she says, and the manner and dedication in which she says them, give proof of her supreme love for her God. How glorious she has often appeared in resolving the many conflicts that occur in our society, procuring for herself a zeal equal to her courage, and a strength of body equal to the wisdom of her counsel."

Thecla, and each of the ten young women, then give a brief summary of their chores and daily reflections. After they have all finished speaking, Arete addresses them by saying, "Having heard all of these moral, upright, virtuous, and sincere young women, I pronounce you all victors, and crown you with the designation 'Respectable Citizen of Seleucia',[8] but for Thecla, as the chief among you, having shone with the greatest luster, I confer the highest designation of 'Honorable Citizen of Seleucia'.

"All the citizens of Seleucia are lucky to have these good neighbors. We have benefitted from their presence, and they, ours. The good people of the hillside cave community should not be ostracized or persecuted, but should be welcomed as equal and valuable members of the greater city and greater Roman community."[9]

After a few congratulatory remarks, the ceremony concluded and everyone returned to their daily routine. They all felt that it was a positive experience for both the community and the city.

THE ASSAULT

THE YEAR is 120 AD. Thecla is 90 years old.

THE healing practices of Thecla and the spiritual community have become well-known and recognized. Many unclean spirits have been cast out by the clan, often accompanied by shrieking noises or uncanny sounds. The families and relatives of those cured have marveled at the power of the spinster Thecla, and many have glorified God for giving her such a gift – and many have converted to the faith.

Because of the sensational and widely-known healing abilities of Thecla and the cave community, the physicians and doctors of Seleucia were being held in a lower esteem than they had been prior to her arrival, because their treatments and cures were just not as effective. The loss of esteem led to the loss of patients, and this brought loss of profit – not good. Things were getting so bad that it was now a serious concern – they became envious of Thecla and her abilities – something had to be done. So, they began to connive among themselves as to how they could rid themselves of the 'virgin priestess in the cave'.

One day, a meeting of doctors was held to address the situation. But alas, the devil was in attendance! With his influence, the group reasoned that since the 'virgin priestess in the cave' was a priestess of the great goddess Diana,[10] and because her virginity was beloved by all the gods, then whatever she requests from Diana is simply granted to her. That must be how she manages to heal so many people. The solution to the problem then became obvious – Thecla would have to lose her virginity – by hook or by crook!

The easiest way to do that, they reasoned, would be to hire a band of thugs for a small sum of money, get them sufficiently drunk, and order them to rape the virgin Thecla by force – with a large bonus payment upon proof of success, of course. Their thinking was that if they were able to debauch the virgin, the gods would no longer love her as much – and if they did not regard her as highly, then Diana wouldn't either – and consequently, Diana would no longer grant Thecla's requests for healing of sick mortals. That was the doctors' devilish plan and rationalization.

And so, they proceeded to carry out the plan. One night, three thugs were hired, drink was administered, and the disreputable crew set off to the community cave dwellings with a seedy demeanor. The doctors smiled contentedly and relaxed, confident that their plan would resolve the problem, and bring wealth back to their practices.

The thugs marched off to the mountain caves with a mission. After finding out which cave belonged to Thecla, they pounded on the makeshift door. But the plan had leaked out, and Thecla had been informed beforehand that ruffians could be coming. Nevertheless, even though she was alone, relying upon the God in whom she believed, Thecla opened the door and said to them politely, "Greetings to you in the name of God. Welcome to our holy community. So, what is your business here?"

They replied, "Are you the one who is called Thecla?"

"What do you want with her? She answered.

"We just want to talk to her," they said in an unconvincing and self-congratulatory manner.

And the blessed Thecla then responded, "Though I am a humble woman, I am a servant of the Most High God and my Lord Jesus Christ; and I perceive that you may not be completely truthful. If you have vile designs against me, you should know that you will not be able to see them through, and you will be punished in the end."

"Ha!" they replied. "You can't stop us from doing anything – we can do whatever we please! There is no way that one frail old prude can fight off three vicious marauders. Woman, give yourself to us!" And while they were saying this, they barged in, grabbed her, and were about to push her down.

But in a calm mild manner, she said to them, "Young men, have patience and see the glory of the Lord."

Then, she looked up to heaven and prayed loudly, "O my most reverend beloved God, to Whom none can be likened – Who makes Yourself glorious over Your enemies – Who delivered me from the fire, and did not give me up to Thamyris or to Alexander – Who delivered me from the wild beasts and preserved me in the water ditch – Who has everywhere been my helper, and Whose name I have glorified: Now I ask that You also deliver me from the hands of these shameful and dishonorable men – and that my chastity, which I have always preserved for Your honor, not be lost. For I love You with all my heart, long for You and worship You, O Father, Son, and Holy Spirit, forevermore. Amen."

Then came a booming voice from heaven saying,[11] "Fear not, Thecla, my faithful servant, for I am with you. Look and see the place which is opened for you. There will be your eternal resting place, and there you will receive the beatific vision."

Then there was a dreadful cracking noise, and the blessed Thecla looked at the cave wall to see the rock begin to rip, and open up a slit about five feet tall from the ground.[12] The crack continued to widen until it was just wide enough for a small person to squeeze into. Thecla immediately realized that this was God's gift of an escape route from the despicable crew. And so, without hesitation, she bravely squirmed away from the brute's clutches and fled right into the crack in the rock.[13]

The thug grasped at her as she was fleeing, and tore off a piece of her veil.[14] But once inside the rock, the crack quickly closed, and there was no longer any visible sign of Thecla, or where the crack once had been. Astonished, the men stood motionless for a moment, staring at each other. Then, they paced around the cave for a time, waiting for her to reappear somehow. After an hour or so, they concluded that she must be dead, either from suffocation or from crushing, so they gave up and left the cave community, a disconsolate lot, and returned to the city.

THE FINAL CURTAIN

AT first, the disappearance of Thecla was a surprise and heartbreaking news for most of the city residents. But the members of the community were not dejected – they knew what had happened – she had gone to be with God. Since Thecla had been previously informed about the contemptible plan, she had told her close friends about it – and told them not to worry because she would be protected by God. Of course, the story that the three thugs subsequently told to the doctors that hired them quickly leaked out, and became headline news throughout the city. Everyone then knew the truth of what had happened.

The blessed Thecla had been saved by her God. And even though her God was not a Roman god, the legend of Thecla spread throughout the region. The cave of Thecla quickly became a holy site – a place oft visited by people from all over the region, wanting to pay their respects to the blessed spiritual and physical healer – the virgin who had challenged the status-quo, overcome persecution and suffering, traveled with the Apostle Paul, and established a community of faith in Seleucia. Over the years, many people were converted to Christ, a church and pilgrimage site were established, and the hillside cave dwellers continued to thrive as a monastic community of faith for both men and women for many years – and the grace of our Lord Jesus Christ was with them all.

This ends the story of the life and suffering of the first female martyr and missionary of God – the virgin Thecla – who came from the city of Iconium at 18 years of age. Afterwards, partly in journeys and travels, and partly with a monastic cave-dwelling community, she lived for 72 years, so that she was 90 years old when the Lord took her.

The day which is kept sacred to her memory is the 23rd of September,[15] to the glory of the Father, and the Son, and the Holy Spirit, now and for evermore. Amen.

NOTES

1. It was said that Thecla 'illuminated many in the word of God'. This was interpreted by many early Christian scholars (Gregory of Nazianzus, Gregory of Nyssa, Eusebius, Methodius, Athanasius, John Chrysostom, Justin Martyr, etc.) to mean that she 'baptized' people. Now, it is generally believed that in the beginning of Christianity in Asia Minor, such things as women preaching, or women baptizing, had in fact happened, since this was a time when ecclesiastical affairs had not yet taken a definite form. Whether Thecla actually 'baptized' anyone is unknown.

2. Unbeknown to Thecla, Paul may have already died. The best records available today indicate that he was executed in Rome sometime between 62 and 64 AD.

3. Compare with Jesus' retort in Matthew 4:8-11.

4. Detractors called it the 'Jesus cult', 'cult of the Nazarene', or just simply a cult.

5. Arete had to tread a thin line here. Roman officials were not enthusiastic about strange cults that preached things not in congruence with Roman traditions, laws, and behavior. But, as long as she kept 'under the radar', it was unlikely that there would be any repercussions. In any case, local Roman political jurisdictions usually had their own local rules about the handling of cults. And here in Cilicia, they had a wide tolerance. There were many such cults – in fact, the local indigenous people had a very strange language and religion – but they were tolerated by the Romans as long as they didn't flaunt Roman authority.

6. The community was not exactly a nunnery – there were a handful of male members in residence.

7. Arete didn't really understand the Christian religion. But she recognized that a god was involved and that unseen forces associated with that god existed in the world.

8. Of course, no such official title existed (although Arete may have wished that there was one) – it was just a ceremonial label.

9. Arete may have been trying to nip in the bud, what she perceived as a possible future persecution by the city's influential political or business elite.

10. Diana was the Roman goddess of fertility (Artemis was the equivalent Greek goddess) and was strongly associated with the woodlands and forest creatures. Furthermore, the worship of Diana was associated with the lower classes, which the doctors of Seleucia considered the cave-dwellers to be. Altogether, this might explain the choice of this deity by the doctors. In Roman art, she is commonly depicted as a huntress with bow and arrow.

11. The hoodlums also heard the voice, but had no idea what it meant – nor did they care.

12. The wall was only about 6 feet from where Thecla and the thug were standing.

13. The thug wasn't holding her too tightly, not being very concerned that she could actually get away from them all.

14. This was by the permission of God. The shred of veil would remain for all future visitors to see – as a confirmation of what happened to the blessed Thecla. That very spot in the cave would become venerated, and convey blessings in succeeding ages to all those who would believe in the power and mercy of the Lord Jesus Christ.

15. Saint Thecla is venerated in the Roman Catholic, Eastern Orthodox, Episcopal, and Coptic religious traditions. Her Feast Day (Day of Holy Commemoration) is September 23 in the Catholic and Episcopal rites, and September 24 in the Eastern Orthodox and Coptic rites.

EPILOGUE

The End of the Story

JUST when you thought it was over!
Not so fast, dear reader. There is one tidbit more of the story to be told.

THE YEAR is 120 AD.
THE PLACE is in the rock wall tomb of the cave residence of the blessed Thecla in the hills on the outskirts of Seleucia.

AFTER a few moments of quiet and stillness within the rock wall of the cave, Thecla's mind and spirit entered the presence of God, and she received God's message:

Thecla, my devoted servant, you have been stalwart in the faith amidst the greatest of suffering and persecution. The unbelievers and evil doers who wanted to have you killed, so that their ego would be satisfied and their status be raised, will be cast into the Gehenna of fire – and will see you sitting above them. They will be sorely grieved and will gnash their teeth – but they are condemned forever! But I tell you now, I will set you on a throne above your adversaries, and I will transform you to the glory of divine heavenly existence.

Then, with her remaining breath, Thecla said her final prayer: "O great God in Whom all perfections are infinite, I adore, praise, glorify, and love You. My heart overflows at the contemplation of Your beauty and splendor. I rejoice that You are so perfect and holy, and I desire to participate in Your perfections to the degree that will give You the most glory.

"O almighty, everlasting, and unchangeable God, creator of heaven and earth, and of all things visible and invisible, I acknowledge in You a true and indivisible Trinity of Will, Word, and Wisdom, with unity of substance. I glorify You, my most compassionate Lord, my sweetest hope, my dearest light, my joy, and my life. I am sorry for my sins with all my heart. I have sinned against You, whom I should love above all things. To Your most sacred majesty I now wholly devote myself, and to Your divine grace will I resign and yield myself eternally.

"Lord, Master, God of all virtue, I ask that You not estrange me from the body of Paul, my dearest friend and esteemed teacher from the beginning. But allow me to be buried near his body, even though I am a sinner and unworthy, so that my soul will be at peace.

"O my beloved God, to Your most merciful goodness – into Your hands I now commend my body, my soul, and my spirit. All glory and honor are Yours, now and forever. Amen."

With that, Thecla's strength begins to ebb, and she drifts off into semi-conscious sleep. A few minutes later, her limbs become loose, her hands and feet lose all power, her mouth becomes dumb, and her tongue ceases altogether to speak. She closes her eyes and silently gives up the ghost.

The life-force of Thecla ceases and she breathes her last. A trumpet is sounded from heaven, and a multitude of angels representing the angelic hierarchy, cry aloud in a mournful voice, saying: "Blessed be the glory of the Lord and the works of His making, for He has favored Thecla, the creature made in His image." After the angels had spoken these words, an Angel of the Seraphim with six wings snatched Thecla up and carried her off to the Crystal Sea, washed her thrice in the presence of God, and then returned her back to earth.[1] In this manner, the sleep of the dead was consecrated.[2]

God then commanded the heraldic angels to assemble in His presence, each according to its order. And all the angels assembled, some having censers in their hands, and others having trumpets. Then, the Word of God and the Spirit of God,[3] accompanied by the cherubim and all the angels assembled, were carried on four winds down to the earth where the body of Thecla was lain in the rock.

At the proper time, the Almighty God, sitting on His Holy Throne, stretched out His hand and began the process of taking away Thecla's soul and spirit. He handed the task over to the Archangel Gabriel saying, "Let her be in your charge until the day of Judgment, until the last days when I will convert all sorrow into joy. Then she will sit on a throne higher than all those who thought they should be higher than her. Now hear this! Lift her up into the Third Heaven, and leave her there until the day of Judgment, when her body will be resurrected."[4]

Then Gabriel took Thecla's soul and spirit, and left them where God had said. And all the angels sang glorious hymns of praise, marveling at the fate of Thecla.

Now, it so happens that Episteme and Therasia, long-time co-workers and companions in the cave-dwelling fellowship community, have come to Thecla's cave that very evening to check on her well-being. Finding it open and empty, they were concerned, and knelt down to pray for her welfare.

As they prayed aloud on their knees, unaware of the heavenly presence within the wall, the Archangel Michael appeared and said to them, "Episteme and Therasia, rise up from your penitence and prayer, step outside and Behold! – your friend and fellow believer in God has gone out of her body! Look up and witness her spirit being borne aloft to be before her Maker. Gaze up into the heavens and I will 'open' your eyes."

As the two believers rose up, wiping the tears off their faces, they looked upward and saw a glorious sight: a chariot of blazing colors carried aloft by four bright eagles, and with a host of Seraphim angels preceding the chariot. When the host came to the place where Thecla's soul and spirit were lying, they halted in reverence, and a multitude of heraldic angels began to appear between Thecla and the chariot, carrying golden censers containing burning frankincense. All the angels came in haste to blow upon the incense, and in short order the smoke filled the Third Heaven. Then, all the angels fell down and worshipped God, praising Him aloud saying, "Holy God, Holy Mighty One, have mercy on Your child Thecla, for she is in Your image, and is the work of Your holy creation."

Seeing these fearful wonders in the presence of God, Episteme and Therasia wept out of both joy and fear. They could see with their own eyes the Third Heaven being opened – the soul and spirit of Thecla being raised heavenward – and all the holy angels praying on her behalf. They spread the story throughout the community.

After this, the Archangel Michael asked what should be done concerning the laying out of the consecrated, but pre-resurrected, bodily remains. God then spoke to him, saying "Go now to the earth to retrieve the body and carry it to the catacombs in Rome. The last wish of the blessed Thecla was to have her body laid near that of Paul, champion of the faith and ambassador to the world. There was a bond between them, the bond should continue, and the forces of hell shall not prevail against it."

Michael did as instructed, embalmed the body, and laid it in a fresh tomb not far from the resting place of Paul.[5]

Thus, Thecla's wish to travel to Rome to be with Paul was fulfilled.[6]

This ends the story of Saint Thecla.
And now you know the rest of the story.[7]

NOTES

---

1. The Crystal Sea is also referred to as the Acherusian Lake.

2. This process only takes a fraction of an earthly second, too fast to be noticed by anyone attending to the body (although many people have reported a spiritual 'flashing' or 'passing' sensation at the moment).

3. The Second and Third Persons of the Holy Trinity.

4. The doctrine of a Future Life, and the teachings of consecration, resurrection, and the final Judgment, are clear here – as is also the doctrine concerning the intermediate abode of departed souls in the third of the seven heavens. Many Roman Catholics believe that this is now the place of Purgatory.

5. In Roman times, distance over the ground was traditionally measured by long poles or rods (stadia) laid successively end to end. Saint Thecla is buried 2-3 stadia (1214 – 1890 ft) or (405 – 630 yards) from Saint Paul's tomb. The distance is because Thecla's tomb is in the Vatican City catacombs, whereas Paul's tomb is in the Papal Basilica of Saint Paul Outside the Walls (known as St.-Paul's-Outside-the-Walls).

In June 2010, Vatican archaeologists of the Pontifical Commission for Sacred Archaeology, using laser technology to remove layers of clay and lime rind, discovered a frescoed portrait of Saint Paul the Apostle, on a wall of the 'Catacomb of Saint Thecla' in Rome, lending credence to the story that her body had been miraculously transported from Seleucia to Rome, to be close to Paul. The portrait, dating from the late 4th century, is believed to be the oldest image in existence of Paul.

In 2009, fragments of bone which had been kept in an underground sarcophagus for over 1600 years, were identified as the remains of Saint Paul. Pope Benedict XVI said scientific tests confirmed that shards found in the underground chamber at St.-Paul's-Outside-the-Walls were from the apostle. Paul's tomb is below a marble tombstone in the basilica's crypt, about 4.5 feet below the altar. The tombstone bears the Latin inscription *to Paul the apostle and martyr*.

After his death, Paul was buried in the family tomb of a devout Roman noblewoman, Matrona Lucilla. In 320 AD, the Emperor Constantine built the first small basilica to receive the pilgrims visiting Saint Paul's tomb. In 390, the Emperor Theodosius enlarged the building and encased Paul's remains in a sarcophagus located on view in the middle of the church. In 433, part of the building collapsed during an earthquake. In the course of renovations, the floor was elevated, and the sarcophagus was buried, covered by a marble tombstone. In 1823, a fire completely destroyed the ancient basilica, and the modern St.-Paul's-Outside-the-Walls was built on the site. The main altar, named the Papal Altar, was placed over the sarcophagus and tombstone, which had been covered by concrete and debris. Starting in 2002, workers and archeologists opened a window

28" wide and 39" deep through the concrete layer under the main altar to reach the side of the sarcophagus. Today, pilgrims visiting the basilica can see the side of the sarcophagus through a small window that was left open under the papal altar.

6. as voiced by Thecla when in Myra, and as written in her letter to Paul from Seleucia

7. The signature tag line sign-off of Paul Harvey and his widely listened-to radio program *The Rest of the Story*, which aired from 1952 to 2008, reaching up to 24 million people a week.

POSTSCRIPT

Commentary

ANCIENT REACTIONS

IN the early Christian Church, Saint Thecla was seen as a heroine and role model, who eschewed the social and pagan norms of the Roman Empire, and chose to follow the teachings of the Apostle Paul – despite persecution.

Her commitment to Paul's teachings, particularly her disavowal of marriage, led her to actions that were considered revolutionary, and her countercultural stance set her at odds with the Roman authorities. Yet her fierce determination and faithfulness were celebrated by many in the early Church, leading her to become one of the most popular female saints of early Christianity. Eventually, this perspective would infiltrate into the greater Roman Empire.

Many women across Asia Minor, Egypt, and Europe became enamored with the story, personality, and life-choices of Thecla. She was praised among them as a sort of patron of empowerment for women – and a culture of imitation began to emerge.[1] Several of them would live together in chastity and celibacy in households, hermitages, and sometimes in monastic adjuncts. These women would often travel together as bands of empowered suffragists, telling stories of Thecla and her grace. Other women in the group would name their daughters after her, and engrave her face on their tombs and oil lamps. All of these women did things that not many women would ever dare to do, and they built a strong community in which they empowered each other.

But her popularity was not always in a positive light. There were many who spoke out against her and tried to denigrate her actions. In fact, efforts were made to debunk the whole story as a mere fiction written by a disgruntled church worker.[2] However, the consensus of opinion today is that the story is credible but unsubstantiated (it is classified as apocrypha or pseudepigrapha).

Rejecting the 'blessedness' of motherhood for future rewards in a foreign kingdom was threatening to an empire that prided itself on establishing peace for the whole world (the 'Pax Romana'). It was seen as subversive. The Romans didn't take kindly to subversives or spies working for a foreign land that could possibly be an enemy waiting to pounce. In any case, for the empire to survive and thrive, it needed children.

In the Roman world, 'good girls' became mothers. Becoming a mother, bearing children that survived (ideally sons) for her husband and for the stability of the household, was essential to being a 'good wife'. In fact, many ancient philosophers and medical authors believed that motherhood was a woman's sole purpose in creation.

Thecla's behavior was threatening to the cultural values of honor and shame, and the importance of female chastity in maintaining those values in the ancient Mediterranean context.

In first century Anatolia, the norms of society were threatened when itinerant preachers, such as Paul, rambled on about controversial topics such as: gods, resurrection, good and evil, or faith spreading – as well as the more mundane issues of mixed-sex worshipping, refraining from marriage, equality between men and women, public ministry for women, etc., etc. Regarding these issues in this area of the world, society really hasn't changed all that much.

In a culture where one's possibilities in life were largely predetermined by class, wealth, and gender, asceticism could be seen as a discipline that allowed for some form of individual control. Even if people could not change the political, social, or economic structures of the world, they could change their behavior. Especially for women, a life of celibacy delivered them from some of the undesirable constraints normally imposed upon them. A life of virginity also meant that the risks of childbirth were avoided. Ancient women suffered from complications at childbirth far more often than is the case for women in industrialized countries today. Lastly, celibate women had opportunities for meaningful work and service usually not available to married women.

Within the story, Thecla's role made a great deal of sense to many people because the main message of Paul's preaching was that people should remain pure in anticipation of the resurrection. Of course, the definition of 'purity' is at the core of the message. When the definition is taken in its narrowest sense, this meant that (in some cases) young women were renouncing potential husbands and young men were renouncing potential wives. Of course, there were always conflicting circumstances involved, but this particular message of asceticism is what got Thecla notoriety. She chose to 'say no' to men who weren't used to being rebuffed. And they didn't handle it well. Though she was miraculously rescued from retribution, the fact remains that she defied the societal expectations at will. This message was extremely popular among women at the time, which might also explain why some of the early Church Fathers frowned upon it.

In Paul's teaching about marriage and the life of women, he does not actually forbid marriage, but seems to prefer celibacy to marriage. In his letter to the Corinthians, he suggests that "A man does well not to marry. But because there is so much immorality, every man should have his own wife, and every woman should have her own husband."[3] He then adds, "Considering the present distress, I think it is better for a man to stay as he is. Do you have a wife? Then don't try to get rid of her. Are you unmarried? Then don't look for a wife."[4] Paul's basic message was that dedicated celibacy and virginity anticipate the life of glory after the resurrection, when marriage will no longer exist [5]– which is coming soon – so it would be well to get ready for it.

In any case, the early Christian missionary movement allowed women to minister in meetings, exercise the gifts of the Holy Spirit, and assume leadership opportunities when they met in private houses.[6] Thecla was one of these women who was liberated, seizing the opportunity to embrace a different lifestyle by remaining unmarried, and by entering into a ministry to preach the gospel.

MODERN REACTIONS

Contemporary readers of Thecla's story typically have mixed reactions to it. On the one hand, they appreciate Thecla's strong faith in the face of death and her portrayal as a female evangelist/missionary. But the story's insistence on celibacy is not attractive to most modern readers. Nevertheless, in the ancient world such a lifestyle held strong appeal to many people.

There are 5 other significant concerns about the Thecla story that have caused controversy over the years:

1) Her martyrdom is questionable because she never, in fact, was killed defending the faith – yet she is well known as the first female martyr in Christianity (or proto-martyr in Eastern Orthodoxy). There were multiple murder attempts throughout her life, but God saved her through each, because He saw that she had a strong faith. But if we take the definition of a martyr to be something like: 'One fully intending to give up one's life in defense of the faith under pejorative and deadly circumstances', then the status claim holds.

2) There are some ambiguities between the Thecla account and the canonical Pauline texts. For example, Paul (or someone writing as Paul) specifically commands that he does not "permit a woman to act as teacher, or in any way to have authority over a man, she must be quiet."[7] Yet in Thecla's case, he was the one who directly commanded her to spread the gospel. She not only walks alongside Paul as an equal, but she spreads the faith on her own throughout most of her lifetime. It may be that 1) the writer of 1 Timothy was not actually Paul, and he was just slipping in his own pet peeves. Or, 2) the context of the passage may have an effect on its meaning, such as being locally targeted and not general or universal. Specifically, it may pertain only to some people in the faith community at Ephesus, which had experienced some problems and wayward leanings, and Paul was giving advice to Timothy on how to keep the precepts of the faith in that community under duress. Or the restriction may have pertained only to liturgical or official church activities in general, since women were allowed to minister in meetings and to exercise leadership outside of these areas.

3) There are questions regarding Thecla's femininity. She cuts her hair short and alters her garments to appear as a man. And she seems to have no maternal instinct. Was she the first to 'self-identify' her sexual orientation, as is popular today? Probably not. Her strong sense of helping and nurturing others through healing and counseling could be classified as feminine qualities. But more likely, her behavior could simply be understood as 'a woman must become *manly* to be allowed to refuse marriage and pursue a public career'. This opened possibilities for imagination and action among women in the early centuries of the Christian Church when the tale was told and the text of it was circulated.

4) Her self-baptism has sparked much controversy – not only the legitimacy of self-baptism, but also the practice of women baptizing, in general. It was (and still is) believed by many that this behavior went against the precepts of the church. And so, attempts were made to discredit the story as nothing more than a made-up account – just a fiction of someone's imagination. In fact, the renowned Christian scholar Tertullian[8] complained that some Christians in Alexandria were using the example of Thecla to legitimize the role of women teaching and baptizing in the church. In a famous treatise,[9] he wrote: "But if any defend those things which have been rashly ascribed to Paul, under the example of Thecla, so as to give license to women to teach and baptize, let them know that the presbyter in Asia, who compiled the account, as it were, under the title of Paul, accumulating of his own store, being convicted of what he had done, and confessing that he had done it out of love to Paul, was removed from his place."

However, there were many Greek and Latin scholars who mentioned Thecla by name, and in such a manner as to lead to the supposition that the story is true.[10] It should also be noted that Thecla's acts were not singularly performed. There are ancient records that, in the beginning of Christianity in Asia Minor, such things as women preaching or women baptizing, had often happened in various degrees and forms. The fact of the matter is that this was a time in which ecclesiastical affairs had not yet taken a definitive form.

5) Was Thecla actually in love with Paul? The closet older-man-younger-woman romance was just as popular in the first century as it is today – probably more so. Older men dreamed of the allure and innocence of the younger woman, and young women dreamed of the financial stability and status of the older man – it was almost like the harlequin romance of today. To all ages, it was intriguing, especially when an apostle and a martyr were involved. No wonder the story was so broadly popularized! However, there is not a hint of any such romance in any other Christian writing, canon or otherwise. So, either Paul and his companions were incredibly discreet so as to avoid any leakage, or there really was no outward romance. Of course, Thecla might have been secretly inwardly in love with Paul, but that is forever unknown – ripe material for gossip and speculation, however.

NOTES

1. sometimes called the cult of Saint Thecla

2. Some of the detractors have suggested that a Montanist writer by the name of Leucius was the real author of the story. The implication was that Leucius was trying to popularize Thecla, because of her Montanist practices of celibacy and preaching. Montanism was a popular heretical movement that arose in Phrygia (not far from the region in the Thecla story), in the second century. The essential principle was that the Paraclete (the Spirit of Truth), whom Jesus had promised was coming in the Gospel of John, was now manifesting himself to the world through particular prophets and prophetesses. They deliberately induced themselves in a trance – a kind of ecstatic madness – and then maintained that the words they spoke were the voice of the Spirit. They claimed to have the final revelation of the Holy Spirit.

The most illustrious convert to Montanism was the Christian scholar Tertullian (although he wasn't firm on all of its tenets), who eventually broke with the Catholic church in 212-213 AD. The destruction of the Phrygian core of the Montanist sect was tragic. After they were banned by a decree from the Emperor Justinian, they committed suicide by locking themselves in their churches and then burning them down.

3. 1 Corinthians 7:1-2.

4. 1 Corinthians 7:26-27.

5. Reference Matthew 22:30.

6. Women who were active in the faith and the Church (although not foundational apostles like Paul or the 'saints' in Jerusalem) included:
Phoebe –
    deaconess of the church at Cenchrae
Priscilla (wife of Aquila) –
    co-worker in service to Christ; risked her life for Paul
Mary –
    worked hard for the Roman Christians
Tryphaena and Tryphosa –
    worked hard for the Lord (Romans 16:1-15)
Euodia and Syntyche –
    struggled with Paul in promoting the Gospel (Philippians 4:2-3)
Lois and Eunice –
    instructed Timothy in the Holy Scriptures (2 Timothy 1:5)

7. 1 Timothy 2:12

8. See Note 1 above.

9. Tertullian, "On Baptism" [Rev. S. Thelwall, trans.], chap. 17, *The Early Church Fathers and Other Works* (Edinburgh, Scotland: Wm. B. Eerdmans Pub. Co., 1867). Digital version by The Electronic Bible Society, Dallas, TX.

10. Cyprian, Eusebius, Epiphanius, Augustine, Gregory Nazianzen, John Chrysostom, and Severus Sulpitius, who all lived in the fourth century, mention Thecla, or refer to her history. Basil of Seleucia wrote the text, originally called *The Life of the Holy Martyr Thecla of Iconium, Equal to the Apostles.*

APPENDIX

History and Archeology

LOCATED about 1.55 miles south of the center of the modern day Turkish city of Silifke (which is close to what in ancient times was called Seleucia Cilicia, Seleucia Isauria, or Seleucia on the Calycadnus), archaeologists have found a huge richly decorated basilica,[1] as well as other shrines, all in honor of Saint Thekla.[2] According to many modern biblical scholars, the transcription of the story from oral tradition into text, was accomplished sometime between 165 and 195 AD.[3] This site is the traditional location of her established ministry.

The beginnings of the site are unclear. Up to 312 AD, Thecla's cave was a secret pilgrimage site for Christians and interested visitors. In 374, the site was visited by the respected church official Gregory of Nazianzus.[4] In 384, a woman named Egeria, widely regarded to be the author of a detailed account of a pilgrimage to the Holy Land,[5] visited the site. She mentioned numerous monastic cells (small caves) for men and women on a hill, along with a central surface church encircled by a protective wall decorated with colorful mosaics.[6] In her diary, she recorded that:[7]

(The shrine to) Saint Thecla is situated outside the city on a small hill ... about 1500 paces (away) [8]... there are very many cells on the hill ... in the midst of it, a great wall, which encloses the church containing the very beautiful shrine.

In the late fourth century, the cave was enlarged and given the shape of an underground church. The reused building material shows that there was once a Roman structure there, probably associated with a pagan shrine. The actual shrine of Thecla was relocated from the hill, now called 'Meryemlik',[9] into the cave which was purported to be her home. The grave in the cave supposedly belongs to her.

A more prominent church, called the Church of Saint Thecla, or Holy Thecla's Church ('Ayatekla' in Turkish), was built on the hill over the cave by the Byzantine (Eastern Roman) Emperor 'Zeno the Isaurian' (who reigned 474–475 and 476–491).[10] At its heyday, the church was ~180 feet long x 121 feet wide. It had three aisles lined with 15 columns each, and was then the largest church in Cilicia.

The fourth to the sixth centuries were the height of Thecla's popularity,[11] which was largely concentrated in Asia Minor in the region between Antioch Pisidia and Seleucia.[12] The Emperor Justinian I (reigned 527–565) built a church in her memory at Constantinople.

The site was revered and consistently occupied as a place of pilgrimage and monastic community throughout Byzantine history, until invaded by the Turks in the 15th century.

Today, the archeological site measures ~2625 feet (~1/2 mile) x 2297 feet. Within the site are the ruins of churches, cisterns,[13] baths, and aqueduct fragments. The only standing elements are a section of the apse from the great sanctuary of Zeno's church,[14] and a large community cistern to the north. The cistern is rectangular with a thick enclosure, and was originally fed by aqueduct in addition to rain.

The cave itself remains, and the underground church inside the cave bears instances of masonry dating to the first century. The cave is accessed by descending several steps. The chapel inside has a rectangular plan, ~59 feet x 39 feet. It consists of a nave and two aisles separated by rows of Doric columns. Evidence, such as a small column decorated with a crudely carved woman's head bearing the name 'Thekla', along with a chi-rho cross,[15] indicates that at least one Thekla of that time was a Christian.

Admission to the site is free, but since the perimeter is secured by a fence, it is only accessible during operating hours when the gate is open and attendants are available (usually 9-12 AM and 1³⁰-6 PM).[16] Christian services are held in the cave chapel every year in September, on or near her celebrated Feast Day.[17]

It has been said that it is one of the best attested sites in Christian antiquity. The continuous occupation from the first century until the Muslim Conquest, coupled with the patronage and backing of distinguished leaders, argues for the presence of a thriving ministry. Furthermore, the consistent attachment to the site of the same feminine name indicates the involvement of a strong woman leader in the early Christianization of the people in the area around Seleucia.

The ancient ruins stand as mute testimony to a remarkable woman.

NOTES

1. The major church of influence in the area was usually called 'basilica'.

2. In the Eastern Roman Empire, 'Thecla' was traditionally spelled with the letter 'k' instead of 'c'.

3. McClintock and Strong Biblical Cyclopedia

4. Saint Gregory of Nazianzus (329 – 388 AD), called 'The Theologian', was one of the 4 great doctors of the east (the others being Basil the Great, John Chrysostom, and Athanasius the Great) and one of the 3 Cappadocian Fathers (the others being Basil and Gregory of Nyssa). Throughout his life, he was one of the great champions of Orthodoxy. In 374, he settled in Seleucia in Isauria and visited Thecla's church. In 381, he became bishop of Constantinople and pastor of the great Church of the Hagia Sophia. He organized the second ecumenical council that met there (known as the First Council of Constantinople) and supported the development of the Nicene Creed. He is famous for his *Five Theological Orations*, defending the full humanity of Christ against the Arian and Apollinarian heresies (which denied the full divinity or full humanity of Jesus).

5. Egeria (also called Etheria) was a fourth century well-to-do Christian woman (possible a nun), from Normandy (or possibly Gaul or Galicia) who undertook an arduous 3-year pilgrimage trip to Egypt, Palestine, Syria, and Asia Minor. She kept copious notes in a diary, the information in which was sent in a letter to female acquaintances. It is the earliest extant explicit account of a Christian pilgrimage.

6. The wall was built to guard the church against the indigenous people (called the Isauri) who were considered very malicious, committing frequent acts of robbery.

7. The text is a narrative written at the end of Egeria's journey from notes she recorded en-route in her diary. Known originally as *Aetheria's Pilgrimage* (*Peregrinatio Aetheriae*) or *Egeriae's Travel Notes* (*Itinerarium Egeriae*), the text was discovered in 1884. The letter is addressed to a group of women, and also to an ecclesiastic or imperial official; and is written in a familiar style of vulgar Latin. Two modern English translations are: John Wilkinson, *Egeria's Travels*, (Oxford: Aris & Phillips, 2006) or M.L. McClure and C.L. Feltoe (ed. & trans.), *The Pilgrimage of Etheria*, (London: Society for Promoting Christian Knowledge [New York: The MacMillan Company], 1919).

8. approximately 1.35 miles

9. 'Meryemlik' roughly translates to 'like a place of the Virgin Mary'

10. The story is that Thecla appeared to Zeno in a dream after he had abdicated the imperial throne over political intrigue, and assured him that he would soon recover it. After he did finally ascend to power again, the grateful emperor founded a noble and sumptuous church in Seleucia as a memorial to the famous martyr Thecla – and bestowed upon it very noble endowments.

11. By the third century, Thecla was greatly esteemed. In his first address against Julian the Apostate, Gregory of Nazianzus included Thecla within a catalogue of apostles, and disciples of apostles. Gregory of Nyssa spoke of her as Paul's disciple, and a virgin martyr. Epiphanius put Thecla by the side of John the Baptist and Mary, the Virgin Mother of Christ.

12. The story also flourished for a time in various parts of western Europe.

13. The cistern is a waterproof receptacle built for catching and holding rainwater or water from an aqueduct. Waterproof lime plaster cisterns were common in Anatolia and the Levant during the first century.

14. The apse is a semicircular recess covered by a half dome – universally adopted by the early Christians as the climax of their church.

15. The Chi-Rho is one of the earliest forms of Christogram, formed by superimposing the first two letters of the Greek word for 'Christ' (Christos) in such a way that the vertical stroke of the rho intersects the center of the chi.

Significantly, the Chi-Rho symbol was used by the Roman general Constantine as part of a military standard. Constantine had dreamed of putting a heavenly divine symbol on the shields of his soldiers. The day after the symbol was affixed, Constantine's army engaged the forces of Maxentius at the Battle of Milvian Bridge outside Rome. Constantine was decisively victorious, became Emperor of Rome (306-337), abolished persecution of Christians, and became the torchbearer for Christianity in the Empire.

16. generally one hour earlier in winter

17. Saint Thecla is venerated in the Roman Catholic, Eastern Orthodox, Episcopal, and Coptic religious traditions. Her Feast Day (Day of Holy Commemoration) is September 23 in the Catholic and Episcopal rites, and September 24 in the Eastern Orthodox and Coptic rites. However, the scheduled date of church services may differ, so checking beforehand is advised.

REFERENCES

Literary References:

- Stephen J. Davis, *The Cult of Saint Thecla: A Tradition of Women's Piety in Late Antiquity*. Oxford Early Christian Studies (Oxford: Oxford University Press, 2001)

- Bart D. Ehrman, *Lost Christianities: The Battles for Scripture and the Faiths We Never Knew* (Oxford: Oxford University Press, 2005)

- Edgar Johnson Goodspeed, *The Book of Thekla* (Chicago: The University of Chicago Press, 1901)

- Scott Fitzgerald Johnson, *The Life and Miracles of Thekla: A Literary Study*. Hellenic studies Vol. 13 (Washington, DC: Center for Hellenic Studies, Trustees for Harvard Univ., 2006).

Internet References:

- New World Encyclopedia, https://www.newworldencyclopedia.org/entry/Acts_of_Paul_and_Thecla

- Biblical-Ephesus, http://biblicalephesus.com/about-st-paul/journeys-of-st-paul/story-of-paul-and-thecla

- McClintock and Strong Biblical Cyclopedia, https://www.biblicalcyclopedia.com/T/thecla-and-paul.html

- Bible Hub, https://biblehub.com/library/unknown/acts_of_paul_and_thecla/acts_of_paul_and_thecla.htm

- WGBH Educational Foundation, http://www.pbs.org/wgbh/pages/frontline/shows/religion/maps/primary/thecla.html

- WikiSource, https://en.wikisource.org/wiki/Acts_of_Paul_and_Thecla_(Jeremiah_Jones_translation)

The Legacy of Saint Thecla

- First female Christian missionary and evangelist
- First female Christian martyr
- First Christian feminist, defying societal expectations of the day
- First Christian hermitess and ascetic

  - one of the most popular female saints of early Christianity
  - authorized to spread the Gospel by Saint Paul
  - stood upright and head-high amid oppression and persecution
  - stalwart in faith through suffering and torture
  - blessed with inner strength to preach and minister
  - blessed with power to heal spiritual and physical ailments
  - moved faith forward beyond social and cultural boundaries
  - broke tradition and overcame barriers
  - spread the Gospel with fervor, devotion, zeal, and passion
  - became a folk hero among the young people of the day

About the Author:

Edward N Brown is a storyteller. With a background in science, philosophy, engineering, and theology, he can masterfully blend, like few others, the interesting nuggets of history, fiction, biography, design, romance, poetry, and personal drama – all wrapped up into one delightful easy-reading tale! Years of personal study exploring the great mysteries that connect the secular with the spiritual, coupled with an educational background of three advanced degrees (two MS and a PhD) with a focus on systems thinking, have contributed to his insights on Humanity, Divinity, Reality, and Christianity. The result is a speculative fusion that will both entertain and inform readers of all ages.

Crystal Sea Press website: http://www.crystalseapress.com
Crystal Sea Press email: rystalse@crystalseapress.com
Amazon Author Page:
  https://www.amazon.com/author/crystalseapress_enbrown
Goodreads Profile Page:
  https://www.goodreads.com/author/show/19232863.Edward_N_Brown
Facebook Publisher Page:
  https://www.facebook.com/Crystal-Sea-Press-106797100691990/

Other Books by Edward N Brown

The Passion of Eve: Remembering the End
  • 2020 Original Edition

The Passion of Eve: Remembering the Beginning
  • 2020 Revised Edition

The Passion of Eve: Remembering the Beginning
  • 2019 Original Edition

(all books available in Paperback and e-Book formats)

"I AM the ALPHA and the OMEGA," says the Lord God,
"the One who is and who was and who is to come,
the Almighty!"
"I AM the ALPHA and the OMEGA, the First and the Last,
the Beginning and the End!
Blessed are they who wash their robes so as to have free
access to the Tree of Life ..."

Revelation 1:8 and 22:13-14

www.ingramcontent.com/pod-product-compliance
Lightning Source LLC
Chambersburg PA
CBHW022028170626
46808CB00003B/1104